# The Woman in White

*...and other tales of murder, mystery and adventure*

*By*

**J P Kerawala**

*Illustrations*

Jishu Dev Malakar

UNICORN BOOKS

*Publishers*
**UNICORN BOOKS Pvt. Ltd.**, New Delhi-110002
*E-mail:* unicornbooks@vsnl.com
*Website:* www.unicornbooks.in • www.kidscorner.in

***Distributors***
**Pustak Mahal**, Delhi
J-3/16 , Daryaganj, New Delhi-110002
☎ 23276539, 23272783, 23272784 • *Fax:* 011-23260518
*E-mail:* info@pustakmahal.com • *Website:* www.pustakmahal.com

***Sales Centres***
10-B, Netaji Subhash Marg, Daryaganj, New Delhi-110002
☎ 23268292, 23268293, 23279900 • *Fax:* 011-23280567
*E-mail:* rapidexdelhi@indiatimes.com

***Branch Offices***
**Bangalore:** ☎ 22234025
*E-mail*: pmblr@sancharnet.in • pustak@sancharnet.in
**Mumbai:** ☎ 22010941
*E-mail*: rapidex@bom5.vsnl.net.in
**Patna:** ☎ 3094193 • *Telefax:* 0612-2302719
*E-mail*: rapidexptn@rediffmail.com
**Hyderabad:** *Telefax:* 040-24737290
*E-mail*: pustakmahalhyd@yahoo.co.in



ISBN 81-780-6073-6

**Edition : 2006**



***Printed at :*** United Colour Offset, Delhi

# Contents

*By the Same Author*

The Witches of Waitiki

# 1

# Much Ado About Nothing

"Do you know she's coming to town?"

"Yes, I've heard about it. But when, I still don't know."

"Next week, but just for a day. Are you going to see her?"

"Of course! The whole town will be there."

Krishna was hearing the exchange of words between his mother and her brother, Vijay Uncle. His head swinging from one end to the other like a pendulum, Krishna tried to follow what they were talking about. The three were sitting together for lunch, but the other two obviously thought there was no third person present.

"When was the last time she was in India?" asked his mother, reaching for the salad dish. Krishna, sitting in the middle, passed it on to her.

"They took her away in 1850, I believe. Krishna could you please put a couple of potatoes in my plate?" Vijay Uncle pushed his plate forward and a confused Krishna obliged. 1850? Not his cup of tea.

"I believe she is still as beautiful as ever. Could you please pass the salt son?" Krishna passed the salt to his mother. Beautiful? Now that sounded interesting to the 15-year-old.

"Aha! And they say she will remain as beautiful even a thousand years from now."

Krishna's eyes almost popped out with this piece of information. Exasperated, he asked, "Who in God's name are you both talking about? You know no one can live for a thousand years, let alone stay beautiful!"

His mother and uncle stopped eating and stared at him, as though noticing him for the first time.

"We are talking about the Kohinoor diamond, the greatest, most priceless diamond in the world," Vijay Uncle answered coolly. "The British Royal Government has given permission for it to be exhibited in India, the land of her origin. It will be on display in Pune, next week. Haven't you heard about it? Now be a good boy and give me some of that chutney."

"Well then, why are you using the pronoun 'she'? A diamond is an 'it'!"

"'Kohinoor' means 'mountain of light'," explained his mother with a far-out look in her eyes. "That sounds so mystical, it has to be feminine."

The logic was lost on Krishna as he continued wearing a scowl. Cheesed off at having missed the subject under discussion entirely, he vented his anger on the location of his chair at the table. "And this is the last time I am sitting in the middle. You both have half-finished your meal and I haven't even started, serving you two all the time."

His mother's glowering eyes warned him his protest was out of place, so he quickly returned to the topic of discussion.

"Isn't it risky, taking it around all over the country? What if it gets stolen?"

"Oh, no need to worry about that. She will be protected better than even VIPs. Security systems from both nations will ensure her safety. Plus a local jeweller has volunteered to arrange for the entire electronic safety system. So you see, no one is going to touch her."

The misleading pronoun was getting on Krishna's nerves and he regretted returning to the subject.

"You know Queen Victoria took the beautiful stone to England with her way back in 1850, and it has remained there since, properly embedded in the Royal Crown of the British Monarchy."

"Who took what where?" Karishma, Krishna's inquisitive, tomboyish sister walked into the dining room and slumped heavily on to the chair facing Krishna. "Pass the rice!" she called out to her brother abruptly.

"Queen Victoria, herself," commented Krishna dryly, passing the bowl of rice. "You know, from tomorrow I'll have my lunch after you all have finished."

"I wouldn't do that if I were you," advised Karishma, taking a particularly large helping and throwing a quick glance towards their uncle. He was secretly called 'Cherry Blossom' by the siblings because of his habit of 'polishing' off all the dishes served on the table. "So," she turned to her mother, "who took what where?"

After the Kohinoor news was conveyed to her, which she absorbed most intently, she simply commented, "Interesting."

"How come a piece of stone has become interesting for you?" Krishna asked, not resisting the temptation to pass a snide remark at her. "Generally it is a gruesome murder or a mass killing that scintillates you."

"When a priceless jewel makes an appearance, murderers and thieves can't be far behind."

*****

The next Saturday afternoon found the Patil family in a long queue outside Tilak Smarak Mandir on the busy and crowded Tilak Road. It was April, and Pune is no paradise during that month. There were a number of policemen swarming the place, controlling and keeping a watchful eye on the large crowd.

"Five more minutes in the sun and you'll see smoke coming out of my head. I am absolutely roasted!" grumbled Krishna, trying to fit into the shadow created by his father. "Nothing, not even the world's largest diamond is worth this trouble. Why couldn't we have come in the evening?"

"In the evening the queue will be twice as long. Anyway, we'll soon be in the shade of the hall."

Once within the shade of the hall they all breathed a sigh of relief. The Kohinoor was on display behind a massive glass partition where the imposing statue of Lokmanya Tilak was also seated. For security reasons, only ten people at a time were permitted within the partitioned room. The rest of the queue wound like a snake several times within the large hall, spilling out into the courtyard, and finally out on to the road itself.

"Stop looking at everyone so suspiciously," Krishna sniggered, seeing his sister darting dirty looks at any rough-looking person. "Mum says it will be impossible for anyone to pinch that stone."

Annoyed, Karishma tried to look around the hall more casually, but her eyes still didn't miss a single unusual detail. How could she relax on a momentous occasion like this? The diamond was sure to lure all the crooks in town and she had to be ready. There were at least two-dozen policemen in the hall, all busy with their own duties. But none paying attention to any of her suspects, Karishma noticed. And she had lined up seven possible suspects already.

There were quite a few local VIPs too. There was the chairman of a large industrial house, a local political bigwig, an owner of a leading jewellery chain of shops, and even some socialites. But Karishma was not interested in them. She was busy scrutinising her seven suspects. Every now and then she would excuse herself from the queue, investigate her suspect from close quarters, and return. By the time it was their turn to enter the partitioned room where the Kohinoor was kept, she had narrowed down her list to just two. One was close to them, while the other, though not in the queue, was still some distance behind them.

Inside the glass enclosure, surprisingly, the security comprised just three guards, all armed and standing vigilant around the marble table where the Kohinoor dazzled. It was in a sealed glass case and protected by a series of electronic systems. Lots of 'ooohs' and 'aaahs' were heard from their group of ten, that is, a group of nine, since Karishma seemed least interested in the diamond. All her attention was on the young man whom she had short-listed as a suspect. She noticed his unusually keen interest in the security system surrounding the diamond. She was by now certain he was up to something no good. At one point he looked directly at her and caught her observing him.

Later, when their group was led out through a separate exit, she stayed close to him. Out in the streets, he once again caught her eye and unbelievingly smiled. Karishma found herself off-guard and quickly retreated behind her father. Outside, as they waited for an auto-rickshaw, the young man too stood alongside. Another quick glance and she caught him winking at her.

"Oh no, a wrong number!" she sighed regretfully. She saw him sidling up to her and almost panicked. "Now how do I get rid of him? And I still have to check up on my second suspect."

She managed to give him the slip somehow. Then she convinced her parents that she wanted to stay back, as she had spied one of her classmates.

Alone, she returned to the long queue and found the second suspect in exactly the same spot, out of the queue, as she had seen him earlier. He was around 40 years old, a little heavy at the waist and wore a disgruntled look on his face. Karishma studied him from afar and was soon convinced that this man was not just killing time. His clothes were shabby, his hair dishevelled and he was continuously smoking. He seemed to be scrutinising every person in front of him, and was quite familiar with all the security personnel. Every now and then he left his post and walked around the building, studying all the doors and windows. Karishma stuck close to him, sensing he could be about to make his movc.

Twice the man whirled around unexpectedly and twice found her hovering next to him.

"He knows I am on his tail," thought Karishma excitedly. Keeping him in sight, she pretended to talk with strangers. She spent time with two teen-aged girls and merrily chatted with a talkative old man. Next to the old man was a tall and slim person in a red checked shirt who obviously was a non-Puneite. He wanted to know the shortest route from there to Central Hotel in the Camp area. The talkative old man elaborately explained five 'shortest' routes and was in the process of explaining the sixth option, when the flustered man politely thanked him and went and stood at the tail end of the queue.

When Karishma reverted her attention towards her suspect, he was gone. Quickly she went looking all round for him, but he was nowhere in sight. Had he completed his survey and left? Gosh, this meant she was on the right track after all. Frantically she looked around for a senior police officer.

"I'd better inform the police what kind of man to look out for." She noticed a senior officer and was about to speak to him when she saw her suspect again... with two policemen.

*****

"But... but... how was I supposed to know he was a policeman in plainclothes?" stammered Karishma in front of her father. It was early night and they were at the local police station, where Karishma was being held. "I... th... thought he was prowling around, waiting for a chance to snatch the diamond."

Her father's brother, who was also in the police force, helped in getting her released. But he too was angry at the indiscretion on the part of his niece. "You know, one of these days you're going to get hurt, poking your nose in police affairs."

"We are there to do our job," confirmed the flabby Officer-in-Charge, looking cool and confident. "That place is so well guarded, even a mouse couldn't enter without our knowledge, let alone a gangster. So stop worrying about the Kohinoor, since it is as safe as a..."

Just then the door burst open and a constable charged in.

*"Sir, the Kohinoor is gone!"* he announced breathlessly.

"Where?" asked the O.C. stupidly. And when he finally realised what had just been announced, he jumped up from his chair and screamed, *"WHAT!!"*

*****

"Ha, ha, ha! And thus ended the promising career of Miss Patil, the girl Sherlock Holmes of Pune... ha, ha, ha!" laughed Krishna heartily the next morning, upon hearing the details of his sister's misadventure. "So what's the next step? Charge the Prime Minister with being a spy? Ha, ha, ha!"

"Oh shut up!" said Karishma sullenly and left the room, newspaper under her arm. This had to be the most embarrassing time of her life. And knowing Krishna, its effects would last long after she had forgotten about it.

Upstairs, in the sanctity of her own room, she heaved a deep sigh of relief and settled down to read the details of the theft. Apparently, the heist took place immediately after the place was shut down for the night. Nobody could say exactly when the theft occurred, and nobody saw the thieves. At 8 p.m. when they shut the place, it was there. When the 9 o'clock team went for a check, it was gone.

"It has to be one of the visitors during the day," the officer in charge of the local police station was quoted. "He must have somehow stayed back in the room unnoticed, pinched the stone and... and... got away. No, we don't know how he got away either, as everything was locked from the outside and all the locks were found intact. And yes, the electronic devices protecting the stone were still functioning."

Ah, a case fit for her hero, the great Sherlock Holmes himself, thought Karishma. How would he have approached the case, she wondered. Probably by first investigating the scene of crime itself, she concluded. Alas, she did not have that luxury. If the police caught her anywhere near that area, she feared, they'd probably lock her up and throw away the keys.

"Though we do have one remote clue," Karishma continued reading the OC's report. "We have identified one of the visitors, which our hidden camera caught – Nitin Shah, the notorious jewel thief of Nasik. He was in disguise, wearing a red checked shirt..."

Karishma threw aside the newspaper and charged out of her room and the house.

*****

Central Hotel! That's where the man in the red checked shirt was, she remembered. However, it appeared the police were searching for a needle in a haystack. They had spread out all over the city, sealed all exits and raided every likely joint, looking for him.

Karishma was thinking as fast as she was pedalling her bicycle. Should she tip off the police? With her recent blunder, it was unlikely she would even be heard. But if they did take her word for it, and raided Central Hotel, and did not find their man there – quite likely – then she would really be in a soup. No, she decided, it would be better to check if the man was there first.

She reached the hotel in a sweat and parked herself on the opposite footpath. She saw a lot of movement in and out of the hotel, but nobody's appearance was even close to her quarry. She tried recognising him from the few who looked out of the hotel windows, but the result was again negative. She walked up and down the length and breadth of the building, but her man was nowhere in sight.

Giving up the waiting game, Karishma decided to attack head-on. She walked towards the hotel entrance purposefully, but stopped short halfway. Leaving the hotel was a tall, fat man with a big bushy moustache and wearing a blue shirt. Karishma would have missed him but for his height. That made her give him a second look, and she was convinced. It was the man in the red checked shirt she had seen the day before in the queue. And since he had put on the added disguise of the moustache and the belly, it must be the man the police were looking for... Nitin Shah.

"Good!" she congratulated herself. "Now to inform the police... but where is he going? Is he trying to escape? I must follow him."

To avoid being recognised, she did what half of the Pune women who rode two-wheelers did. She covered her head and most of the face with her *dupatta*. With only the eyes showing, they could all be in the running for the role of 'the bandit queen'. For the first ten minutes it was easy following him, as he walked and she cycled behind him. Then he took an auto-rickshaw.

Cyclists in Pune are a breed by themselves. They actually overtake anything on wheels; whizzing in and out of heavy traffic with such impudence, as though the road belonged to them and the rest were trespassers. And while following the auto-rickshaw, Karishma did not let down this noted tradition.

The chase led Karishma out of the Camp area and into the city area. This is the older section of Pune that is always crowded. The auto-rickshaw had to slow down due to the heavy traffic, and following her prey became easier for Karishma. Soon they passed Rasta Peth and Raviwar Peth, and the chase ended at Narayan Peth.

On paying off the auto-rickshaw, the tall man walked ahead for five minutes and stopped in front of an old building. There was a large, bright showroom on the ground floor. The name read 'M P Jewellers' – this was their main branch.

Karishma's heart pounded as she made the connection. Presumably, Shah was here to sell the diamond. The owner of the shop was Mr M P Jain, a prominent Pune socialite. They say he had more money than the three leading industrialists of Pune put together. If Nitin Shah wanted to sell his diamond, there was no better address in the country for him to do so.

"Jain would probably buy it cheap, sit on it for sometime and when things cooled down, smuggle it out of the country and sell it at a very good price," Karishma made her own conclusions. "But what am I supposed to do?" she panicked once more. "Bring in the police?" She already knew the problem with that.

Five minutes later, after checking out the area, the tall man entered the shop. A minute thereafter, Karishma followed suit.

*****

Inside the posh, air-conditioned showroom Shah was talking to one of the counter salesmen.

"Sorry Sir, Mr Jain will not see anyone today."

"Tell him I am an old acquaintance," said Shah in a steely voice.

"But Sir, I told you he is in a..."

"Just tell him!"

If Phantom's voice could freeze the blood of the most hardened criminal, Shah's voice was chilly enough to freeze the salesman's blood. Standing close by still totally covered in her *dupatta*, Karishma saw the salesman hurrying to the back office with a frightened backward glance.

"Yes madam, anything for you?" another salesman approached Karishma with a big smile.

"I am with him," muttered Karishma softly, pointing towards Shah. The salesman disappeared disappointed, and Karishma casually sidled up closer to Mr Shah.

Minutes later, a short, podgy, almost bald man walked out of the back office door, looking impatient and agitated. He looked around the counter, confused. The first salesman pointed to Shah.

Jain walked hesitatingly towards Shah. "Er... you were looking for me... I... I don't think I know you." He blinked almost continuously as he looked up at the tall man.

"Think again," said Shah, removing the bushy moustache for a split second.

*"Oh... it's you!!"* White-faced, Mr Jain took several steps backward. He stared at the tall man, hand clasped to his mouth in disbelief. "Wh... what are you doing here?"

"I know what you did yesterday... and I know how!" said the tall man softly. He might as well have bellowed, considering the shocking effect it had on Mr Jain.

"I... I... don't know... wha... what you are... talking about..." Beads of perspiration suddenly appeared on Mr Jain's forehead, despite the air-conditioner.

"I want my cut... 25 per cent. Or else..." The chill in the tall man's voice had returned.

"WH... WHAT?? Are you crazy!"

No answer from the tall man. Of course, not because he didn't know the answer, but because silence obviously spoke louder than words here.

"Co... come inside," said a very disturbed Mr Jain. "We'll talk it over."

Mr Jain opened the door to his office wide and Karishma took a quick look at the interior. It seemed sparsely furnished with a single large table in the middle of the room. Sitting in front of the table was the smallest man she had ever seen.

*****

Karishma's mind was in a whir as she stepped out of the jewellery showroom. What was going on, she just couldn't fathom. 'I know what you did yesterday... and I know how!' 'I want my cut!' What could it all mean?

If Shah had come to sell the diamond, as she had earlier guessed, he would not get a cut, he would give a cut. Had she misinterpreted the entire scenario?

Soon Nitin Shah came out of the shop, looking quite satisfied. Karishma followed him back to the hotel and watched him go in. Now what? Should she go to the police? But she was even more confused now than an hour earlier. She dare not implicate an important man like Mr MP Jain without proper evidence.

Back to the scene of crime, she decided.

*****

Tilak Smarak Mandir was a hub of activity when she reached it. Besides policemen and the forensic team, Press and TV journalists filled the place. Karishma spotted the plainclothes policemen who had arrested her the day before. She quickly ensured the *dupatta* was covering every inch of her face. But how do I get in, she wondered.

"You are here again?" A voice shot out from behind her.

Karishma jumped up in fright but was relieved to see her uncle who was a police inspector.

"Uncle! Ho... how did you recognise me?" she asked nervously, taking off the *dupatta* from her face.

"You are my niece, aren't you? I'd recognise you if you were in armour with a full helmet over your face. But why are you here? Haven't you troubled your parents enough yesterday?"

He was looking rather cross and Karishma was too scared to cook up an excuse.

"Well, I'm sorry but I'll have to complain about this to your father," he said. "Come into the hall with me. The telephone is somewhere there."

She was glad she could get into the hall, but how was she going to get out of this trouble? Luckily somebody else was using the phone and she found the time to come up with an excuse.

"Actually Uncle, I came to apologise to the constable who went through so much trouble yesterday because of me."

Her uncle looked at her bewildered, then relieved. "Why didn't you say so in the first place? That was a nice gesture indeed. I think he is somewhere outside. So hop along and apologise to him."

"Thank you Uncle," she said, but instead of walking out she kept behind him as he entered the glass enclosure where the Kohinoor was displayed till the day before. She tried to take in as many details as possible in the short span of time she knew she'd be there. The enclosure now held just the statue of Lokmanya Tilak and the marble table behind it. Gone was the glass case within which the diamond was kept, gone were all the electronic systems protecting the diamond and, of course, gone was the diamond.

"Where are all the protective devices?" she asked aloud.

"They were returned to..." began her uncle. "WHAT?? You are still here?? I thought I told you..."

"I know, I know, Uncle," she quickly said. "I just wanted to invite you home for dinner tonight."

"Oh," her uncle looked puzzled but soon happily agreed to go. A dinner for a bachelor at the Patil's residence was something to look forward to. "Well thank you, that would be nice. Now if you..."

"Good! So where have all the electronic devices gone?" she asked again.

"If you must know," her uncle was sounding annoyed again, "they belonged to one of our local jewellers. He had obligingly lent it to us for a day, and they were returned this morning."

"I see," she said, sounding interested. She was about to ask the name of the jeweller when something aroused her... or at least its absence aroused her interest.

"Wasn't there something else in this enclosure yesterday that isn't here now?"

"Yes! The diamond!" her uncle said impatiently. "Now will you please..."

"No, no, Uncle. Besides the diamond and the case and the devices, I am sure there was something else in this enclosure, yesterday." She tried picturing what she had seen the day before and felt sure there was something else, but just couldn't place it. "What else was here, Uncle?"

Her uncle seemed about to burst. With controlled temper, he slowly said, "For the last time Karishma, the diamond was here yesterday, and it's stolen! The glass case and the electronic system were here yesterday and they've been packed into the wooden box and delivered to the jewellers this morning. THERE WAS NOTHING ELSE!!"

Bingo! The wooden box! There was a large wooden box in a corner, the day before.

"And was the jeweller, M P Jewellers?"

"Yes... but..."

"Thank you, Uncle. See you at dinner tonight." She hurriedly left the enclosure and the hall seconds before her uncle could physically throw her out.

*****

Karishma was piecing together all the information she had collected to date, as she cycled back homewards. Her concentration was so acute that twice she almost got into an accident, and once she actually ran into a pedestrian. She had to form a logical chain of events that must have taken place yesterday, before she could come to a decision. By the time she reached home, she did have a theory that accounted for all the facts and events. But to prove that theory she needed help.

"Krishna!! How nice to see you at home!" She cried happily upon seeing her brother in the hall, reading.

Krishna raised his eyebrows, deliberated, and replied, "Sorry. No favours from me."

"Favours? Who wants favours? I am happy today Krishna, and I want to buy you a gift."

Krishna's eyebrows arched still higher. He deliberated some more and said firmly, "No thank you. I am happy the way I am too, so I don't want any gifts from you."

"Don't be silly. You know that macho steel bracelet you like? I know where they are available and I want to buy you one. So let's go together and get the right size."

Krishna shut his book but didn't get up. He studied every word she said, checked all their possible double meanings and probed all the sticky situations they could lead to. Nothing! It all sounded innocent and genuine enough.

"And what would I have to do for it?" he asked, still suspicious, knowing nothing came free from his sister.

She looked hurt and asked, "Don't you trust me?"

He wanted to answer, but simply got up and said, "Okay, let's go."

*****

"Narayan Peth?" Krishna asked unbelievingly, as she instructed the auto-rickshaw driver. "Why do you want to go so far when the bracelets are available everywhere?"

"I want to give you a special one."

When they got off at M P Jewellers, he was flabbergasted. "But this is an expensive place. Why do..."

"Nothing but the best for my brother," pat came the answer.

Inside the plush showroom she placed her order with a young counter salesman.

"Steel bracelet for men?" he repeated incredulously. "We don't sell steel bracelets here. This is a jewellery shop, you know."

Karishma suddenly raised her voice, "What do you mean this is a jewellery shop? *You think I am a fool?*"

"Here, stop raising your voice," scolded the young man, not realising what he was getting into. "I told you, we don't sell steel bracelets here."

"I saw them yesterday, so where have they gone?"

"You couldn't have seen them yesterday. They weren't there," the salesman tried reasoning.

"WHAT?? YOU'RE CALLING ME A LIAR??" she shouted at the top of her voice. The whole shop went quiet and heads turned towards them.

Krishna, feeling uneasy with the attention, tried to guide his sister out of the shop. Taking her arm, he said, "It's okay, sis, let's go elsewhere. I'm sure..."

*"NO!!"* she screeched. "I SAW THE BRACELET YESTERDAY, AND I WANT IT NOW!!"

The manager of the showroom rushed towards them and enquired what the trouble was. The salesman explained the situation and the manager turned towards her with a smile, "You've got the wrong shop, girl. Maybe you saw it in some other..."

*"GIRL!??* YOU CALLED ME A GIRL!!? *HOW DARE YOU!!"*

The manager gulped hard and immediately started apologising. By now all the customers in the shop had stopped their purchases and were gathering around them. Poor Krishna looked devastated. "What's got into you? Let's get out; it's okay, I don't want the bracelet."

"Yes, do that or I'll call the police," the manager added.

*"POLICE!!?? YOU WANT TO CALL THE POLICE??"* she screamed as never before.

Instantly the backroom office door flung open and the owner Mr M P Jain, rushed out. "Police? Who called the police?"

"THIS MAN DID!" shouted Karishma, pointing to the manager. "IS THIS THE KIND OF SERVICE WE GET OVER HERE?"

The manager quickly explained the problem to Mr Jain. "But we don't keep steel bracelets," began Mr Jain, concerned that some of his customers were starting to walk away. "Maybe, if you come back tomorrow..."

*"BRUSHING ME OFF!!* YOU'RE BRUSHING ME OFF AS THOUGH I'VE COME TO BEG OVER HERE?? WHAT KIND OF..."

"Please Miss, please don't shout," pleaded the owner. "My nerves are already on edge today and..."

"I WANT TO SPEAK TO THE MANAGER!!"

"Miss, I am the owner, and again, I request you to keep your voice down."

"YOU'RE ASKING ME TO SHUT UP??"

"No, no, no! Why don't you come to my office, Miss? Maybe we can sort out this mess."

This was exactly what Karishma wanted and without a backward glance at her brother, she marched towards the owner's office.

The small man she had seen earlier wasn't there now, but the large wooden box she had seen in the corner

of the enclosed section of Tilak Smarak Mandir was very much there. It was to see this very box that Karishma had enacted the whole drama in the showroom. It was about two feet high and three feet by two feet in length and breadth. She guessed that the glass case on the marble table in which the diamond was kept was about a foot high. That figured well with what she had in mind.

"Now please be calm, sit down and tell me what I can do for you," the kindly Mr Jain said as he slumped into his executive chair behind the table.

"I AM NOT GOING TO SIT DOWN!! AND I WANT THE STEEL BRACELET I SAW YESTERDAY!" Karishma was not prepared to quieten down, as she paced the room. When she stood next to the box, she dropped her handkerchief and bent down to pick it up. It was only when her eyes were an inch from the base of the box that she spotted them. Two tiny holes, drilled into the box, two inches above the bottom. With a few more shouting commentaries and a few more trips to the box, she confirmed that the holes existed on all four sides of the box. Her job here was done.

"If that is what will satisfy you," Mr Jain said, "I'll arrange to keep a steel bracelet for you tomorrow. You can come over and..."

"No, thank you," she said sweetly and left the room.

Outside the showroom, she exulted, *"I have it!"*

"What, the bracelet?" asked a confused Krishna.

"No silly... the Kohinoor! And now over to the police."

*****

Later that day Mr Jain, the little man in Jain's office and Nitin Shah were all arrested, and the Kohinoor recovered.

It was late in the evening and the entire Patil family was seated at the police station. The British High Commissioner, who had rushed in from Mumbai, was there too.

"But... but... I still don't understand how you unearthed the entire plot," the baffled Officer-in-Charge of the police station was saying.

"Well, to begin with," began Karishma, who was itching to explain all, "I was once again on the wrong trail. I thought, as you all did, that it was Nitin Shah who had pinched the Kohinoor. But when I overheard his conversation with Mr Jain in the showroom, I realised I was wrong. I still would have been clueless as to who did it and how, if I had not spotted that little man in Mr Jain's office. My process of thinking at that time was that if the hall and the glass enclosure were found sealed from the outside even after the theft was detected, it could only mean that the thief and the diamond were still within the premises. And the only place where it could be hidden, besides the statue, was the wooden box. And how could that be done? The little man gave me the idea that if there was a hidden compartment in the box, a small man like him could somehow squirm into it. And like the Trojan Horse, he now had direct entry into the enclosed area. When the coast was clear he could come out of his hiding place, and do his job. Plus, as he was M P Jain's man, he would also know how to switch off the electronic devices at the time of taking the diamond from the case, and then switching them on again. Once the diamond was with him, he could return to his hiding place and wait to be transported back to his boss's office next morning. Simple and effective, as it turned out.

"But to be sure of the plot I had to first find out if the box was designed to hold a secret compartment. The little holes near the base confirmed they could only be there as ventilators for a stowaway."

"Incredible! Absolutely incredible!" conceded the O.C. "And of course we found the hidden compartment. It was just nine inches high at the base of the box. A false bottom fooled us all."

"But you've got to admit it was a marvellous feat of endurance for the little man to remain inside that box for 36 hours, as the arrangements were made the night before the Kohinoor was displayed," said Karishma's uncle, who had arranged the raids and the arrests.

"We came to know he was a professional contortionist."

"Well, all is well that ends well," concluded the British High Commissioner, rising from his chair. "In any case, it was just as well it was not the original Kohinoor."

There was stunned silence in the room.

"Wh... What do you mean, Sir?" asked a wide-eyed Karishma.

"We thought something like this could happen, so we used an exact copy of the diamond. It is only made of crystal. Of course, the whole thing was top secret."

All that trouble, all that anxiety... for a crystal copy? Karishma silently vowed never to trust the Brits again.

Still in a daze, the family prepared to leave for home. To Karishma's surprise, her policeman uncle came home with them. "Nothing like a good meal at the end of a hard day's work," he said happily, rubbing his hands vigorously. A puzzled smile from her mother, and Karishma remembered her invitation. She had forgotten to keep her mother informed. Another major problem! But Karishma felt she had solved enough for the day, and didn't let the glaring looks from her mother bother her much.

"But why did you tag me along to the jewellers?" asked a harried and still totally confused Krishna. "You managed the show on your own anyhow."

"I was worried I might go too far and they may want to beat me up," confessed a crestfallen Karishma. She was so set on being the heroine of the day, till the British High Commissioner poured cold water over her aspirations.

"So..."

"So with you there, I thought maybe they'd vent their wrath on you, instead of me, a girl."

Krishna looked disbelievingly at her. "And my bracelet? What about my bracelet?"

"What bracelet?"

❑❑❑

## 2

# The Woman in White

"Whew! That chilled me to the bones," said Patrick, thankful to be out in the sunshine again.

"It was okay, I suppose. It was just a movie," Brahma didn't sound impressed.

The two, along with their friends, Amir Ali and Rahul Chaturvedi, had stepped out of a cinema hall showing the horror movie, *Creatures of the Night*.

"Patrick, you will get the chills just seeing the silhouette of an old house against a full moon. This is all hype, and what we saw in the movie simply feeds our imagination," Amir, the born cynic, was always ready to bring his friends down to practical reality.

"I would only partly agree with you there, Amir," corrected Rahul, joining the discussion. "Yes, most of our fears are the work of imagination... but not all. There are some things in this world that are beyond logic."

It was a wintry afternoon and the four decided to walk home and take in the sunshine. Sometimes Delhi winters, particularly during the night, get so chilly that even the old-time seasoned locals get taken by surprise.

Patrick's house was the nearest so that's where they all headed first.

"You were talking of me getting the creeps seeing an old house in the night, well, let me tell you I get the creeps even in daylight when I pass that house," said Patrick, pointing to a house across the street. The two-storeyed house had a large courtyard in front and though not very old, it wasn't well maintained. A short boundary wall cordoned it off and an iron gate was the only entry.

"But isn't it your friend Ronnie Jordan's house?" asked Rahul. "And why are you scared of it? It doesn't look creepy to me."

"Strange sounds come from it occasionally, as though it is haunted, and the neighbours generally avoid it. During some nights they say it is really awful."

The four stopped walking and stood gazing at the house.

"See, this is exactly what I mean," said Amir. "Someday someone perhaps heard a sound from within the house that he couldn't explain. So he called it a 'strange' sound. Immediately it becomes a 'haunted house', and people avoid it. And the night sounds may be due to some other practical reason. But nobody cares to investigate, and the net result is our brave friend Patrick gets the chills every time he walks past it. As I said earlier, imagination runs wild when practical thinking takes a back seat. There must have been a simple source for those 'strange' sounds, but I suppose people like to be thrilled and chilled."

"You think you are so smart and brave? Then why don't you come and 'investigate', as you put it, in the middle of the night?" challenged a visibly agitated Patrick.

"No problem," was Amir's cool response. "I'll be here at nine and stay back till dawn. By the way, who all live in that house?"

"Just Ronnie's mother. I heard Ronnie himself is studying in some school in Shimla, and his sister married and left the city a few months ago." Patrick was now not particularly happy that his friend had taken up this potentially-dangerous challenge. "But how will we know that you actually spent the night here?"

"I'll join him," volunteered Brahma, never to miss any excitement.

"We'll give you a more logical answer by tomorrow morning," promised Amir with a half smile.

*****

"We'll camp here, Brahms, under this tree," suggested Amir as he put down the packet he was carrying. It was almost 10 p.m. and they were in the courtyard of the house with 'strange' sounds.

Brahma too set down his small packet and looked about him hesitatingly. The house was single-storeyed and stood about 50 feet away. Brahma could just about read the name with the help of the streetlamp. It read 'Shubh Niwas'. All the lights within were already switched off, save for a lone bulb burning from one of the windows on the first floor.

Brahma now regretted opening his mouth and volunteering to join Amir. This was not his idea of a pleasant night. It was getting chiller by the minute, and doubts had arisen whether the single blanket each had brought for himself would suffice.

The traffic had trickled down considerably by 11 p.m., and the only sound to keep them company was the continuous buzz of mosquitoes. The blankets were tightly wrapped around them, leaving only a narrow slit open for their eyes.

"Why... are we here?" asked Brahma, eyes heavy with sleep.

"To prove a point. Come on, don't look so bored. This is exciting... take it as an adventure."

"I prefer to have all my adventures and excitement in dreamland, warm and safe in my bed."

Another hour of vigilance, another couple of degrees colder and soon after midnight the solitary light too went off. Shivering, the boys drew closer to each other as they sat resting their backs against the tree trunk. The blankets shielded them from the cold and the insects as well. The traffic now was almost non-existent but the mosquitoes were out in droves.

"See, it's past twelve and no sounds from the house," said Amir softly. "I told you it was all humbug. Another few hours and we can safely..."

Just then a sound came from the house. It was a long moaning sound, and stopped as suddenly as it had started.

"Di... did you hear that?" asked Brahma, jumping to his feet.

Amir had sat up too, trying to analyse the sound he had heard. "Could be the mother," he whispered, not sure of himself at all. "Maybe she is in some kind of pain. Let's sneak up to the window and check."

The two walked up to the house trying their best to remain out of sight. Taking all precautions possible they peeped through all the four windows facing the courtyard.

"Nothing," whispered Brahma, with the first signs of alarm creeping into his voice. "And no one's around either."

"No bedrooms in sight," Amir sounded puzzled too. "The old lady may be sleeping upstairs and yet the sound came from below. Maybe it's the sound of the wind coming through some narrow crack."

Not particularly keen to explore any further, Brahma agreed quickly. "Yeah, maybe. Come, let's go back to the tree."

By one o'clock it was near freezing and the blankets were just not enough. Then an idea struck them. They put the blankets together and shared it. The body warmth and the double blanket helped ease their shivering to an extent.

"Next time somebody has a belief, I won't try to prove him wrong," Brahma promised himself. The sound had left him wide-awake and he kept checking his watch to see how much longer it would be before the sun came up. Amir found the extra warmth comforting and instantly fell asleep, his head on Brahma's shoulder.

Listening to the steady breathing, Brahma too was on the point of dozing off when another sound alerted him. This time it was not a long moaning sound, but short low-pitched ones, like the hooting of an owl, or the call of a lonely pigeon. It sounded very scary. Brahma's temperament could stand it no longer. He nudged Amir to wakefulness and tearing the blanket away from himself, he stood up.

"I've had enough of this! This place is definitely haunted!" he cried out, not caring to lower his voice.

Amir, now standing in a daze too, still couldn't figure out where he was, or what they were supposed to be doing.

"What happened? What happened?"

"Awful sounds came again from the building, you sleeping beauty. Now pick up your blanket and let's get out of here."

Amir hushed him and tried concentrating on the sounds, which had continued, unabated.

"Are you coming, or..."

"Sshhh... I think the sound is of pigeons only."

"You can continue with your guesswork, if you like," said Brahma, folding his blanket. "I am going home."

"Wait a minute, Brahms. We can't leave just like that. If indeed it were the sound of pigeons, we would have proved our point. But we'll have to first prove it."

"You prove it. I am..."

"Don't tell me you are afraid of pigeons?"

"I... of course not! But I'd rather..."

"Come on. It'll take only a minute and then we can go home convinced."

The two once again crept up to the window of the house. The sound was still audible but the pitch had reduced considerably.

"I don't see any pigeons inside," said Brahma softly, as he scanned the dark room from the corner of one of the windows.

"I don't either," confirmed Amir from another window, "but the sound is continuing. Let's go inside."

Amir had to hold on tightly to Brahma to prevent him from running away. But after much arm-twisting and persuasion, he once again convinced Brahma that there was no danger in entering the house. One of the windows was not secured well, so that's the route they took to get inside.

Holding hands tightly (assuring each other it was only so that they wouldn't be separated in the darkness!), they explored the room.

"I c... can... can... st... still hear the s... sound," whispered the trembling Brahma, "and no pi... pi... pigeons?"

Amir was nervous too but he concentrated hard to locate the source of the sound.

"I have a torch," Brahma remembered suddenly. "Shall I put it on?"

"No, not yet. I am still not sure if we are alone."

"Wh... wh... what do you me... mean?"

"That sound is almost human... and it seems to come from..."

*"Look!!"* shouted Brahma, clutching Amir's hand hard and pointing at the doorway between two rooms.

There, just for a split second, stood a figure in white. It seemed to be a woman. And then it vanished.

There was no stopping Brahma thereafter. In another two seconds he had jumped out of the window and was racing towards the gate and onto the road. Amir had raced Brahma many times earlier and both were more or less equally fast. But tonight it was like Michael Greene racing a lamppost. Amir was almost left standing as Brahma streaked out of the house, out onto the main road and away into another street. It was only after five minutes when Amir reached him that he opened his mouth.

"That's that! No more proving points for me."

*****

"I told you both to be careful," admonished Patrick the next morning as the four friends walked towards their school. They narrated the previous night's adventure and both Patrick and Rahul were surprised at the risk the two had taken going into the house.

"That was really too dangerous," commented Rahul. "I think that should teach you both a lesson to let some things alone. Ha, ha, ha! I'm sure you'll never go anywhere near that house again."

"*Au contraire,*" clarified a thoughtful Amir. "I will be going there again, tonight. Alone."

"WHAT??" the other three blurted together.

"You must be crazy!" said Brahma. "Whatever makes you even think of returning to that dreadful place?"

"It was the sound... I thought it came from somewhere below us. Couldn't be pigeons there."

"Of course, there were no pigeons there, you moron. Didn't you see the woman in white? She was making the noise." Brahma was astounded at his friend's naivety.

"Wrong! The sound from below continued when the woman made her appearance. And she was making no sound."

Definitely no sound came from the three friends as they stood still, gaping at Amir.

"So... maybe... there are more women in white," suggested a visibly frightened Brahma.

"I am not sure, but tonight I'll find out." The determined look on Amir's face worried the others.

"Don't be ridiculous!" Rahul tried sounding the man in charge. "This is no kid stuff. We are keeping away from this, and you certainly can't do it alone."

"I can! And I will! There is something not right in that house, and I intend finding out what secrets it holds."

*****

Later that night a more determined Amir entered the courtyard of 'Shubh Niwas', and took his position under the tree. To help him remain awake this time and keep warm, he carried a flask of coffee. Scared, he certainly was not, but some company from one of his friends would have been welcome, he thought ruefully.

But he needn't have worried – a few buildings away, sitting by a roadside teashop, were his three friends.

"We might as well be with him," grumbled Brahma, annoyed with himself for being cajoled into accompanying the other two, for yet another shift of 'night-duty'.

"No, Amir wouldn't want that. We all know how proud he is, so when he says he wants to do it alone, let him do it alone."

"All the same, we'll be nearby in case there is trouble and he needs help," said Patrick, sipping his first cup of tea.

An hour and three cups later, the teashop closed down for the night. "Now let's go to the haunted house," said Rahul, "but we'll remain out on the road, out of sight of Amir. And no more talking."

There was some kind of shelter on the footpath across the road from the house, and the three huddled together under it. They pulled out their blankets and settled down. In the courtyard across the road, they could see the faint silhouette of Amir under the tree. The house again sported a single bulb on the first floor but there was no other movement or sound from inside.

At midnight, the single light went off, and the three friends braced themselves for the ordeal ahead. Twenty more minutes and the long moaning sound became audible. It started softly, almost muffled, but soon became louder and clearer. They saw Amir move slowly towards the building. The three quickly crossed the road and hid behind the boundary wall.

Amir reached one of the windows and peeped inside. Everything seemed to be the same as the night before. Except for, thankfully, the absence of the woman in white. Since the way was clear, should he step in through the window, he wondered. Before he could decide, another sound added on to the long moan. It was the sound of a steady thumping. It also seemed to be coming from below and was not sharp enough to disturb anyone outside. But the three boys on the street heard it.

"What's going on?" asked Patrick, quite alarmed with the eerie atmosphere.

"Couldn't be Ronnie's mother, as the sound is not from the first floor," commented Rahul, studying the building intently.

"It's the woman in white, I tell you," Brahma swallowed hard, ready to beat a hasty retreat if required. "I wish that nutcase Amir would give all this up and return."

But Amir had already prised open the window. Shaking all over, yet adamant to get to the bottom of it all, he hoisted himself on the sill and was about to jump in when he heard a loud rattling sound. It was quite loud and not consistent, but strangely, it came from above him.

"What in God's name is creating that racket?" cried out Rahul, now definitely anxious.

"It's coming from the first floor," said Patrick.

"He's still going in!" exclaimed Brahma, disbelievingly, as they saw Amir jump into the dark room. "That idiot is still going in."

"Okay, enough is enough!" said Rahul, readying to jump over the boundary wall. "Let's go and get him out."

The three jumped over the boundary wall and ran through the courtyard, hearts thumping with excitement and fear. They reached the window even as the sounds continued. They peeped in, but there was no sign of Amir.

"In!" ordered Rahul, scampering onto the sill in one quick movement. "Let's all go in!"

Much to Patrick and Brahma's chagrin, they too climbed into the dark room. Instinctively, the three held each other's hands.

"Wh... where's he?" asked Patrick.

"That's wh... where we saw her... last night," stammered Brahma, pointing to a doorway.

"Give me your torch Brahms." Rahul grabbed the torch and walked briskly towards the doorway. The other two followed without any prompting.

Rahul switched on the torch in the next room and all three let out a sharp yell of horror. All stood transfixed at the sight that greeted them. Amir was on the floor, back against the wall and right hand on the left side of his chest. Standing ten feet in front of him, and in a strange glow of light, was the woman in white.

The torch slipped from Rahul's limp hands and crashed to the floor, plunging the room into darkness, save for the eerie glow from the woman. In the next instant, the glow vanished, and so did the woman.

It was over a minute before the boys could react. They rushed to Amir to make sure he was alright. But Amir sat motionless, staring fixedly at the spot where the woman in white had stood. Rahul grabbed his cold wrist and felt his pulse. It was beating at an incredible pace. He lightly rapped Amir's face and called out softly but urgently, "Amir, get up! Come on, we are getting out of here!"

Amir gave a low groan and shifted his head, relief flooding into him as he saw his friends. They half lifted, half dragged him, and managed to bring him back to the front room, pushed him through the window and out into the courtyard.

All through the frightful moments, the low moaning and the dull thumping continued... with more intensity. They didn't waste any more time in the courtyard either. Picking up Amir's blanket and thermos from under the tree, they scrambled over the boundary wall and stumbled out onto the safety of the road.

"*Wow!*" was Rahul's first reaction.

"Never!! Never again in my whole life do I want to go through anything like that again." Brahma never looked more sincere as he made this solemn declaration.

"I hope you are satisfied now," said Patrick, looking angrily at a more sedate Amir. "You know, you almost got killed there! The way you were clutching your heart, I wonder how you survived."

"I am okay. Yes, I did feel a slight pain there when I suddenly saw her but it's gone now." Compared to the others, Amir looked surprisingly composed. "And no, I am not satisfied with what I saw. In fact, the more I think about what I saw, the more I am convinced that that was no ghost or spirit of any kind."

Three jaws dropped, waist high.

"Wh... what is he talking about?" asked Brahma, looking incredulously at his friends.

"The moment I came face to face with that woman, I saw her making a quick movement to adjust the white cloth over her head. During the sudden movement, something fell on the ground. I think it was a pair of spectacles." Amir related this slowly, as though going through the scene in his mind.

"So?" Brahma was not ready for any kind of explanation, and simply wanted to get back home.

"So how many spooks have you heard of wearing spectacles?"

The boys tried digesting this new piece of information.

"So it's a short-sighted ghost, so what? Must be dozens of them around. Now can we please go home?" Brahma implored.

"I'm going back in!" said Amir flatly.

"And I am not!" insisted Brahma, equally sure of his intentions.

There was another standoff, as the four friends tried reaching a consensus.

"I won't see Amir going in there alone, so I'll accompany him," intervened Rahul. "But promise me this Amir, if we don't find the spectacles, we come out immediately."

"Agreed!"

As the two turned to go back to the house, Patrick decided it would be safer to be with the two than with Brahma, and followed them. Brahma knew he would be safer with the three than by himself and his imagination, and followed suit.

*****

The four stacked their blankets and other items under the tree and stealthily tiptoed their way back to the house and the open window. Four jumpy hearts decided to coordinate with four pairs of terrorised eyes. Every time the eyes spotted something in white, hearts would leap into their mouths.

After the umpteenth false alarm, the four climbed onto the window and into the semi-dark room. The low moaning sound was still audible but the dull thumping had stopped.

"No sign of her yet," said Rahul.

"Yo... you sound as th... though you are complaining," whispered Brahma, at the same time persuading his heart to return to its place.

They slowly crept towards the room where they had found Amir, all set for an emergency. This room too, like the one earlier, was pitch dark. They groped for their torch that Rahul had dropped earlier and found it. A few taps at its base and a white beam burst forth, lighting the room. Rahul shone the torch where the woman in white stood.

"Sorry Amir, no spectacles."

Amir rushed to the spot and scanned the area, but Rahul was right. There were no spectacles.

"Now can we..."

"Oh... oh... oh... noooo! W... we... have... com... com... company, guys," Brahma called out in a strangely sing-song voice. He was pointing to the top of the staircase that they had not noticed earlier. There, looking down at them in silence, were two women in white.

"Now, we've... really... had it! I... I... can't... even run," said Patrick tearfully, rooted to the spot, as all the others were.

All, but Amir. He walked shakily to the foot of the stairs, not taking his eyes off the women for even a second. And then slowly, one step at a time, he started climbing it.

"Wh... what is... he... do... do... doing?" Brahma wanted to know, not daring to run away, and at the same time not daring to even blink.

"Come back Amir," warned Rahul, shifting the torch beam from the women to Amir.

Amir did not respond. As though mesmerised, he kept climbing. Suddenly one of the women raised her hands and cried out eerily, *"Oooooooh!"*

Yet Amir didn't flinch. Though his entire body was tied up in knots, and his mind was swirling as if in a whirlpool, he kept climbing the stairs until he stood one step below the women. Then he reached out and pulled the cloth covering the taller woman's head. Rahul's torch beam caught her face clearly.

*"Good God!!"* exclaimed Patrick. "It's Sally!"

There was stunned silence as the two parties appraised each other. But Patrick's recognition did not ease the tension amongst the other boys.

"And... who's... Sally?" asked Brahma nervously. "Sally, the living; or Sally, the dead?"

"The living, stupid! She is Ronnie's sister. She had married and left the city a few months ago."

Sally was slim and in her early twenties, and as she looked down at the boys she seemed as frightened as them. Then the shorter woman removed the scarf covering her head, showing a kind face, but it looked tensed by two deep lines furrowed between her eyes. She asked quietly, "Who are you boys?"

*"Mrs Jordan??"* Patrick called out in surprise again. "Why are you two hiding your faces? You scared the wits out of us!"

Sally found the light switch and put it on.

"Patrick O'Brien! What in heavens are you doing here? And who are these boys?" cried out the old lady, half angry and half relieved.

"They are my friends, Mrs Jordan. And we came here to investigate the strange sounds we heard. It was only to help you."

"Oh dear," sighed the old lady, sounding totally broken and demoralised. She sat down on the top step. "Why couldn't you mind your own business? Now the whole story will be out."

"What's going on here, Mrs Jordan?" questioned Patrick, now brave enough to climb up the stairs and sit alongside her. "And what are those sounds from your basement?"

The moaning and thumping sounds from below reached a crescendo and the boys once again became nervous and edgy.

"Sounds like someone's there." Amir wiped the sweat dribbling down his forehead.

"Mum, I think it is time to reveal the truth." Sally rubbed her mother's back and shoulders soothingly. Tearfully, Mrs Jordan agreed with a sad nod.

Sally began telling her story. "You see Patrick, sometime around the beginning of this year, Ronnie started acting strangely. At times he would cry for hours, without any proper reason. At other times he would get so agitated, he created a great ruckus, shouting and abusing anyone he met. Sometimes, he would even get violent. All this naturally affected his studies, and as you know, he failed miserably in his exams."

Patrick remembered how everyone was surprised that a clever student like Ronnie could fail. Then came the even more upsetting news that he had been sent to Shimla for further studies. Ronnie had not even met his friends before departing.

"Soon it had become quite apparent," continued Sally, "that Ronnie was losing his sanity."

The news hit Patrick like a bolt of lightning. "WHAT?" He just couldn't believe his ears. "Are... are you sure?"

"Mother was very patient with him, hoping he would somehow snap out of this... this predicament. But his condition worsened. He stopped going out and avoided meeting anyone... not even his close friends, and went into a deep depression."

The four friends heard her with keen anxiety, cringing at the thought that a perfectly normal person could reach such a fate – and for no apparent reason.

"So..." prompted Patrick, anxious to find out what had become of his friend.

"So mother thought he was possessed or something, and took him to a local witch doctor."

Patrick was horrified with what he heard. "*Oh no?!* But as Christians, surely you could have consulted the parish priest? Or even a doctor! A psychiatrist could have helped."

"We tried both, but Ronnie would get more violent at the sight of the parish priest. And the doctor prescribed tranquillisers. Its effects were only temporary." By now, Sally herself was in tears. "The witch doctor was our last hope."

"And did it help?"

"No! He first performed some rites and when that didn't work, he took to beating the 'evil spirit' out of Ronnie." Here both the mother and daughter burst into a tearful cry. Sally continued, "Mother quickly put a stop to that... and..."

"And...?"

"She locked Ronnie in the basement. I was against the idea, and tried dissuading her. But mother was alone with the problem, so she did what she thought proper... keep him out of harm's way."

It took some time for the gravity of the situation to sink into the minds of the boys. They looked at each other for some kind of support, some kind of conviction, acceptable to them.

"You mean..."

"Yes. The sounds you hear are from Ronnie. The moaning sounds are his cries, and the thumping noise is his feeble banging on the door."

The four looked accusingly at Mrs Jordan, their eyes demanding an explanation.

She saw their shocked expressions and through her tears and sobs asked, "What else could I do, boys? It was that, or total humiliation for the family."

"She was worried that my marriage would be in danger if the news spread that my brother was losing his sanity," explained Sally in a choking voice, trying her best to cajole her mother. "I now come here once a month to comfort Ronnie and try to bring him back to his senses."

Unbelievingly, the boys felt no sympathy for them. Their hearts were with another young boy who, like an animal, was cooped up in a cage, sentenced to a life of solitude; for almost a year. He was a young, intelligent and innocent boy deprived of his freedom for no apparent fault of his own.

"But why are you two dressed like that?"

Sally again came to her mother's rescue. "The sounds Ronnie made downstairs attracted attention. Mother had a device upstairs that made a loud rattling noise. She switched it on to drown Ronnie's cries. And if people still came to investigate she would scare them away with this simple guise of covering her face and moving around in the darkness. After you saw me accidentally yesterday, I too put on the same guise. Today I tried making it even more sinister by holding a dim torch under the shawl. But it backfired as, in the process, my spectacles fell off. I had just retrieved them before you all returned."

The boys wondered if this was indeed a pitiful story, or a deviously criminal one.

Rahul brought the matter into proper perspective. "I am sorry ladies, but you know, we'll have to bring the police into this."

*****

Early next morning the police came and arrested Mrs Jordan on charges of mental torture of her son, as well as endangering and causing harm to his life. Later the same day, she was released on bail and a court hearing was fixed. Two weeks later the court found her guilty of the charges, but in view of her age and helplessness, she was given a suspended light sentence.

Sally, who had come over just a day before to help her brother, was allowed to return to her husband.

Ronnie, in an extremely weak condition and a 'shocked' state of mind, was immediately hospitalised. A team of doctors and psychiatrists diagnosed his condition as a minor case of schizophrenia. All it required was regular treatment with specific medication and prolonged therapy with a psychiatrist.

Ronnie's mother and sister listened intently as the doctor counselled them. He said, "Like Ronnie, many youngsters suffer this malady. And they are often misunderstood. Emotionally disturbed children need to be understood and given extra love and affection. It is this neglect that intensifies the emotional disturbance."

In a few months' time, Ronnie recovered and was back to being a normal, sane person. He thereafter left the city and went to stay with his sister.

❑❑❑

# 3

# The Wonder Boy

It was another cloudy morning with promises of frequent, nagging rains. Most residents of Darjeeling preferred to stay indoors and only a few essential shops had cared to open for the day. There was no point for the other shops to open, as there were no tourists around. And no tourists, meant no business. As the town wore a drab, cheerless look, the mood of the citizens was also grumpy and lethargic. That is, of most citizens. I, on the contrary, was full of joy and on a particular high – for I was with Trixy... the apple of my eye, the rainbow in my life and the girl of my dreams.

As you may have already guessed, I am Cocktail, or Cocky the half-breed. I stay with the Pradhan family, made up of Mr and Mrs Pradhan, Vishnu and Divya, and guard their house. I have but one true friend, Raja, the pariah; and one true love, Trixy. It's not a happy triangle, as Raja hates Trixy and her upper class ways and, likewise,

Trixy detests Raja's rough ways. So, I end up passing time with either Trixy or Raja... never, together.

"You know, I would love to meet this Kharga Bahadur," said Trixy as we sat at our favourite place on the wet grass of the slope, above the circular road at Chowrasta. This section was known for the beautiful panoramic view of the Kanchenjunga and the surrounding mountain ranges. On any clear day, the Kanchenjunga seems to actually jut out from the rest of the range, almost inviting you to touch it, even though it could be a hundred miles away. But today we could not see even ten feet from our nose, thanks to the clouds that had enveloped the entire district. Which of course suited us fine, as we wanted the privacy.

I looked at Trixy startled, "And who is this Kharga Bahadur?"

"You know that mysterious boy who has been rescuing all those animals from the zoo?"

"Oh," I was relieved. "But I really wonder if it is all true."

"But it is! You know Rexy? He is from the zoo area. He claims to have seen it with his own eyes."

Rexy was a handsome Alsatian and he occasionally dropped in at the bazaar where most canine friends bumped into each other and exchanged the latest gossip. Of late he bumped into us more often than I cared for. "You know I really wouldn't care to mix with that fellow. There is something about him that..."

"But he is so handsome and commanding and..."

"Yeah, yeah, I know. So what did he see?" said I, brushing aside further adjectives.

"He says this Kharga Bahadur has a special way with all animals. He doesn't talk to them or anything like that. But he somehow understands us and the animals understand him completely. All the animals at the zoo trust him completely, and wouldn't hurt him even when he puts his hands into cages and pats them. They say he has some master keys and on certain nights, he creeps into the zoo and quietly opens the lock of a cage. He then frees the animal and actually walks away with it, out of the grounds. And the authorities have no knowledge of this special bond and are always puzzled when an animal disappears."

"I really don't believe all that Rexy says," said I, frowning at the excitement in her eyes. "What would a boy do with all those wild animals, I'd like to know."

"Rexy says he takes them miles away from the township, and lets them go back to the jungle and their natural habitat."

"Whatever for?"

"Rexy says it's his mission in life."

The regular 'Rexy says' was getting on my nerves.

"And what about the poor zoo? They've actually been robbed of animals. Surely the police will catch this boy. And don't tell me what Rexy says to that. Tell me what you think!"

For just a second her surprised look showed hurt, but she answered, "I think it's better for the animals to be out and free again. Rexy says... er... I think... that is..."

"Hello there!" a voice rang out from below us. It was Rexy. "What are you two doing up there?"

I wanted to say, 'Discussing your views and theories.' But before I could answer, Trixy called out, "Why don't you join us? It's beautiful up here!" In two bounds and a leap he was panting happily next to us. Suddenly the beautiful place turned ordinary and I wanted to leave.

"Well I'll be getting along," said I, getting up. "See you in the evening, Trixy."

"Have you heard the latest?" asked Rexy, forcing me to stop and enquire politely. Just another hoax to gain Trixy's attention, I was sure.

"The locals of Lepcha town have found the skinned carcasses of two leopards, a tiger and four antelopes."

"Wh... what do you mean, 'skinned carcasses'?" Trixy looked horrified.

"They were killed by bullets and then skinned."

*"Oh no!!* How terrible! Who would do such a ghastly thing?"

"Poachers! The value of those skins will run into lakhs. What is mystifying is that the killings took place in more or less the same region. Yes, word from the animal kingdom has it that it is the same area that Kharga Bahadur took his freed animals to."

*****

Tragic and startling as the news was, I didn't stay back to get further details. I left the charged-up Rexy to impress Trixy with the gory details.

I didn't like the direction the day was leading to. There I was a few minutes ago, joyful to the brim, enjoying every moment time had to offer, until... until that macho busybody showed up. I don't understand why he doesn't leave us alone, in spite of my openly showing I don't care for his company.

Anyway, I still had my best friend around to be with. Raja, the sturdy street dog with more battles than he cared to remember behind him, had kind of taken a liking for me and was always there when I needed him... as all good friends should be.

"Hi Cocky!" came his gruff voice as I spotted him trying to find a bone amongst the waste dump, close to where he hung around. "Why the long face?"

I didn't want to tell him about Rexy, as he would immediately put the blame on Trixy. He loved doing that... the one thing I wished he would change.

"Just heard the news about the animals near Lepcha."

"Yes, I heard about it too," he said, trying to open a cellophane bag that showed some leftovers. "A heinous crime, and a shame it had to happen to the animals who had just been freed."

"So it is confirmed they were the same creatures?"

"It figures that way. The very same species of beasts that were freed in the past ten days are the ones that were killed and skinned." There was very little sign of revulsion or remorse on the face of this rugged friend of mine as he relished the chicken skin he found in the cellophane bag.

"You think the boy, Kharga Bahadur, is behind this? Maybe he is the one skinning them or maybe he is getting some cutback."

"I really don't think so. I've met this boy, and he seems to be a genuine friend of animals. Last month he had rescued two bears and nothing has happened to them. But after hearing this news today, I believe he is going to stop the rescue act altogether."

"What a shame," said I, tasting the chicken skin Raja offered. I spat it out immediately, nauseated. It was unwashed and at least a week old. "I would have liked to meet him too."

"So come on," he said, flipping the rest of the skin into his mouth and swallowing it. "I know where he lives... just below the Christian cemetery."

We strolled back the way I had come. It had started drizzling again and absolutely no one was on the road.

"Want to wait till the drizzle stops?" I offered, as the drizzle became heavy.

"Why?" he asked innocently, looking perplexed. Nothing ever bothered him, I knew, but he ought to know cats and dogs don't like water on them. We continued with our walk, totally ignoring the now pelting rain.

Ahead we saw another dog, zigzagging from one shelter to another. It was Trixy, alone.

"There you are," she said cheerfully. "Why did you leave so suddenly?"

"I had to go some place," said I, a bit stiffly. She saw Raja pacing around us impatiently and stiffened too.

"Well, want to drop me home?" she asked with an unsure smile, half knowing the answer.

"Sorry, we are busy."

She carried on homewards without another word, and we carried on our own way. Good. That will teach her I am not just a nobody.

"Bravo!" said Raja, an expression of admiration on his face.

We reached Kharga Bahadur's place shortly. It was in the midst of a *busti* of a few poor people. Again, due to the rains, no one was around except for a beggar sitting a couple of houses away, hiding under a large blue plastic cover. Raja barked aloud a couple of times. Instantly a face appeared in the window of one of the houses. It was a boy. Seeing us, his sad face broke into a hint of a smile.

"It's you, Raja," he said, coming out in the rain. He stroked Raja's head roughly, just the way he liked, and looked at me. "And who's your little friend?" He stroked me under my chin and neck, just where I like it most.

He was about 15 years of age and had an extremely sensitive and ascetic face. And when he looked at me it was with very penetrating eyes, which actually cut through all physical barriers and reached directly into my heart and soul. There was an instant connection and an unexplainable thread of communication was established. No way would this boy harm a creature of the animal kingdom, I knew.

"I know it is about the murdered animals that you've come to find out about," he said looking at both of us. Not a word had been said by either of us, but he knew. A tingling feeling ran through my body and I knew it was no ordinary human being I was sharing the rain with.

"But I have decided to put a stop to rescuing animals from the zoo. How can they trust me any longer to lead them to safety and freedom?" he said, sad eyes mirroring his inner feelings.

That, I felt, was like cutting off the nose to spite the face. He was doing a great service to the animal kingdom, and to stop it because...

"Only till the culprits are caught," he said, looking at me directly. He was actually reading my thoughts. "But who will even try to catch them?" he asked sadly, and walked back into his house.

*****

This Kharga Bahadur left a profound impact on me. After returning home, all day long I brooded over what he had said. 'Who would indeed catch the culprits?' It was common knowledge that some of the authorities had a share in this 'business'. With so much money at stake it is easy to tempt a guard to look the other way. It also is as easy to induce the higher authorities not to conduct a raid or search.

I didn't feel like having lunch, so I skipped it. I was too busy figuring out how such a crisis, such gross injustice, could have befallen the animal kingdom. One does not come across such mass killings in the forests of Darjeeling hills. Poachers get away with hunting an animal

or two, once in a while, such as a stray deer or, rarely, a leopard. But these killings are always deep in the forests, far from any human habitation.

So, I concluded, what Kharga Bahadur's mission offered them was a chance to kill a handful of animals, all in one place, close to home, without even having to actually hunt for them. An opportunity served to them on a silver platter. But to get to the bottom of this affair, I needed to think more logically.

It all came down to one thing. How did they come to know where and when Kharga Bahadur set the animals free? Were they waiting at a particular spot or did they follow him? If they were waiting for him, it meant he had predetermined the place to set the animals free. Possibly, he even spoke about this place to someone. Alternatively, if he had not preplanned the release point, the poachers apparently followed him... but how would they know when he was going to rescue the animals from the zoo? Of the two possibilities, the first scenario seemed more plausible to me.

There was a third alternative, the poachers just happened to be around at the point of release. I discounted this possibility as it seemed rather remote. There had been no such poaching reported from that area for many years.

Later that day, I confided my suspicions to Raja. "If we can learn who Kharga Bahadur had spoken to about his plans, we can track down the poachers."

Dog of action, that's Raja. No wasting time 'thinking' or 'contemplating' over a matter for him. "So let's find out," he said and trotted off towards Kharga Bahadur's house.

"But... how will you ask him?"

"Remember, he can read our minds. At least I hope he does so this time too."

It was late afternoon and very few people were at the Mall. The sun had still not peeped out from behind the dark clouds and I knew that again an entire day would go without it smiling down at us. Thankfully, at least it had stopped raining. We reached the house and noticed the small street deserted too. Raja repeated his morning bark but this time no face appeared at the window. He tried again but it was obvious the boy was not at home.

"What do we do now? Wait for him or..." It started to drizzle and I needed to think no further. Getting wet in the morning had already given me a slight cold.

"We wait," said I and scampered under a parked car.

"Why are we hiding?" asked Raja, joining me. I didn't bother with an answer.

*****

Almost an hour later Kharga Bahadur returned. He was with an elderly lady and both were sharing an umbrella. We waited for the elderly lady to enter the house, and then Raja stepped out in the rain. He gave a soft bark. Instantly Kharga Bahadur was with us, again oblivious of the rain. I remained under the car, with just my head protruding.

"You two again?" he asked, a little apprehensive. "Hope nothing has happened... oh, you want to ask me something?"

It was a bit strange going through my theory mentally, without even a bark. I really had my doubts if he could interpret us, considering our complex and lengthy chain of thoughts. But he was concentrating hard as he searched our eyes with his penetrating ones, and as though we had spoken some simple language, he replied, "No. I have never discussed anything about my special abilities with anyone. And, in fact, I myself did not know where I would be freeing the rescued animals till the last minute."

That stumped me totally, not so much the text of the answer, but his ability to interpret us like an open book. Maybe it was not actual reading of our minds. Maybe, it was something like penetrating and merging with our thought waves. Basically, he understood our thoughts and our feelings and it was a bit scary. I immediately made sure no dirty thoughts entered my mind – it could get embarrassing.

"So that part of your suspicion has gone for a sixer," Raja looked at me dejectedly. "What was the alternative theory?"

"Somebody may have been following him."

"I wouldn't feel sure about that," said Kharga Bahadur immediately, as though I had spoken to him. "I haven't noticed if I am being followed. But I'll keep it in mind in future."

After he left, Raja came back beside me. "Why are we still hiding?" Mind you, it was pouring at that time. "Why can't we go back now?" I raised my eyes in exasperation and looked at him with a bored, resigned expression. "We are the only ones on the street," he observed, "us and that beggar."

I jumped out of my shelter and looked down the street. Sure enough, the same beggar with the same blue plastic sheet was seated in the same place I had noticed him sitting in the morning. Strange, did he come out only during the rains? I told Raja of my suspicion.

"That poor beggar, part of the poacher's gang? *Tchah!!*" he silenced me with contempt. "Now you are letting your imagination get the better of you, little fellow."

"Let's wait and watch." I refuse to be shrugged off so easily.

For two hours we remained sheltered under the car. The rains stopped and started again but the beggar maintained his position. All along, not a single person had offered him alms. It was already dark and time for me to return home. But somebody had to keep watch.

After much protest and temper Raja agreed to stand guard for the night.

"Only until that beggar maintains his post," I reasoned. "And I'll be there to relieve you first thing in the morning."

"What will I get to eat on this Godforsaken street?" he sounded angry as I got up to leave. But he was right. There were no restaurants or hotels or even affluent homes here, whose garbage cans he could rummage through.

"'The best sauce in the world is hunger'," I offered lamely, "and I quote Cervantes."

He looked at me as though I had spoken Greek. "What does that mean?"

I regretted bringing literature into our conversation. "It means that even tasteless food tastes better if taken with sauce. Therefore, if hunger is the best sauce, every dish becomes more appetising when one is hungry." I believe I couldn't have made it easier for him to follow.

He gave a good thought to what I said and replied, "Clever fellow, this Cervantes." Good! I at least taught him something today. "But let Cervantes have his sauce. I am just craving for some juicy bones."

On my way back home I thought I'd drop by to meet Trixy and make amends. She came out slowly when I gave our secret bark and asked frostily, without looking at me, "Yes?"

If the arctic region ever warmed up, all that needed to be done was to send her up there, particularly in this mood, and everything would return to normal. I knew it would be a waste of time trying to warm her up to me today, so I just muttered something and carried on home. Maybe time would heal her wounded pride. I could try again next morning.

*****

But next morning, Trixy seemed in a worse mood. She didn't come out even when I called. Worried that this might escalate into something more serious, I promised myself I'd compromise with her and bring the matter to an end, as soon as I was through with my 'duty hours' at Kharga Bahadur's house.

"What's eating you? Blast it, again I'm thinking of food," was how Raja greeted me. I agreed it must have been a hungry and lonely guard for him last night.

"Any news?" I asked, spotting the beggar in his place.

"I think you've got it all wrong. There's been no trouble at all."

"Wait a minute! That's not the same beggar." I squinted to see better.

"Of course not! Late last night another beggar came in, and the old one gave him his place."

"But that means I was right! Can't you see they are maintaining a watch on Kharga Bahadur."

"Er... maybe. Got anything for me to eat?"

"Sorry. But I'm taking over, so go ahead and find yourself something." Without as much as a 'see you later', he disappeared in a flash.

As the skies temporarily cleared, I snooped around outside the house, and made my way towards the beggar. Wagging my tail as though in a playful mood, I stood in front of him. I hadn't seen this man before. He was clean-shaven, big built, and definitely didn't look a beggar. He had simply covered himself with a dirty cloth, and the same blue plastic sheet was lying near him. I needed no further evidence. The two beggars worked together and definitely, seeking alms was not their profession.

He suddenly picked up a stone and flung it at me, hitting me on my front paw. I yelped and slunk away and returned to my post under the car.

A while later another beggar came along and promptly settled down next to the big built man. They exchanged words and the big man got up and started walking away.

A thought suddenly struck me. I followed him, hoping he'd lead me to their hideout.

I followed him down to the bazaar area, and then through a narrow lane I had never used before. A little later we were once again in the open. The slope here was steeper, with very few houses and no roads at all. Up to now I had taken care not to be caught following him. But in this open area it was difficult to find cover. I looked back and saw half the town looming above me. The other half was covered in grey clouds.

The beggar, now without his dirty cloak, seemed to be absolutely uninterested in his surroundings as he steadily trudged downwards, deep in his own thoughts. We must have covered quite a distance and I regretted not having informed Raja or anyone else of my mission. Suddenly a voice called out from behind.

*"Jeetu!"* The big man in front of me turned around, and so did I. Walking down towards us was a shady-looking young man. "When did you get yourself a dog?"

"I have no dogs!" the big man retorted from below. "You know I hate them."

"Then why is he following you?" asked the young man, catching up with me. "He's been on your tail ever since you left the town."

Oh, ho... problems!

Jeetu, the big beggar, climbed back upwards to check on me. I had two options here, run for my life, but lose the opportunity of tracking down the animal killers, or stay back and convince them that I was just a friendly dog. I chose the latter.

"It's the same dog I saw at Kharga Bahadur's house," he said, looking at me with surprise. I looked back, happily wagging my tail.

"Maybe he likes you a lot."

"Or maybe," said Jeetu, looking at me suspiciously, "he's been made to follow me by that animal lover. Maybe he's on to our game."

"Hmmm..." I heard the other man murmur, "can't take the risk."

Next instant a locomotive engine seemed to have fallen on my head, as something hard and heavy crushed me to the ground. It was an instant journey to oblivion.

*****

When Raja returned to Kharga Bahadur's house, and found Cocky missing, he was not overtly concerned. "Must have been sidetracked by Trixy," he assumed angrily. Moreover, he saw the beggar in his regular place and further assumed all was okay. But when Cocky didn't return after two hours, doubts started creeping in. And when he saw Trixy approaching him alone, he panicked.

"Where is he?" he demanded.

"Cocky?" she asked a little baffled. She too took shelter under a car as it had started raining again. "I thought he'd be here. I wanted to..." she didn't complete her sentence.

"Great Scot!! Where has that scamp disappeared to?" cried Raja, pacing up and down in front of her.

"He is not a scamp!" she corrected him indignantly. "He is hundred times better than the company he keeps." Her nose was up as she refused to even look towards him.

"Don't start fighting with me again or else..."

"Woah, woah! What's all this talk of fighting?" It was Kharga Bahadur, who had come out on hearing the commotion. Trixy had not met Kharga Bahadur before, but on seeing him immediately understood who he was.

"Cocky has disappeared and this little... whatever, wants to fight with me," complained Raja.

"*Whatever??* You called me a whatever?" Trixy was beside herself with anger, as she tried to control her temper.

"Calm down, both of you!" Kharga Bahadur commanded. "What exactly is the problem?"

Raja explained the situation. Even Trixy heard the entire story without interrupting.

"Oh dear, I hope he is alright. And I came over just to..." she once again stopped mid-sentence.

"We are meddling with killers here, so we better move cautiously," warned Kharga. "But how do we proceed?"

"Trixy has a good nose," Raja grudgingly suggested. "Maybe she can pick up his trail."

"Not while it is raining. All scents have been washed away."

"Maybe I can help," offered Kharga. He pursed his lips tightly and sucked in hard, making a loud squeaky sound. A couple of times more and an old rat emerged from a nearby dump. He scampered towards them confidently. Raja was about to pounce on him when Kharga stopped him.

"Stop! He's a friend." Kharga then conversed with the rat in his unique way and announced, "Yes. Cocky has followed the beggar. He went that way towards the bazaar."

"So let's not waste any more time, for unless something has happened to him he wouldn't have taken so much time." Raja was already half on the run.

"Wait! We have no idea where he may be. He could be anywhere in town. I have a better idea." Kharga gave a soft whistle and, unbelievably, a fantail bird flew in. As the two dogs looked on at the astonishing sight of a boy and a bird communicating, a happy thrill ran through them. Soon Kharga turned to them and explained. "He will pass on the message to the other birds. We'll soon know where Cocky is lying, as these birds can fan out quickly and scan the entire town."

"What if Cocky is somewhere indoors?" Trixy asked, concerned.

"Most of that area will be covered too, as sparrows and other house birds will join in the search. Only if he is behind locked doors, and in a room without windows, will it be a problem."

The word must have spread faster than a forest fire, for within ten minutes the skies were full of birds of every shape, size and colour. It was an overwhelming sight for the people of Darjeeling, a sight that will be talked about for years and years, as tens of thousands of birds suddenly left their nests and flew over every nook and corner of the town. From the majestic mountain eagle that flew high and covered the entire town in a single scan, to the ravens and crows that concentrated on narrow roads and by-lanes of the town, to the tiny budgies and sparrows that zoomed in and out of every house and every room. They were all there to answer the call of help, from the boy who, they now realised, was more than just someone who understood animals.

It was not long before the report came in. "Cocky is not in town!"

"Then look for him outside the town," was the next command. In a couple of minutes the town was barren of every bird, as the people saw them fly outwards purposefully.

The news came in faster this time.

"They found him! He is lying motionless on the way to Purohit village."

"Before we leave, take care of that beggar. He'll surely follow Kharga," reminded Trixy.

"Leave him to me," assured Raja. "You two go ahead, I'll catch up with you soon."

Raja next did, what he did best... intimidate. Standing in front of the beggar he presented a picture of horror... fangs in full view, snarling and growling... hair standing on the back of his neck and shoulder, poised as though about to attack. The beggar sat rooted to the ground, not daring to even blink as the fiery eyes hypnotised him. He remained in that position long after Raja left him.

It took 15 minutes of steady running for Kharga Bahadur, Trixy and Raja, who had caught up with them, to reach the half-dead, drenched body of Cocky. They were helped all along the way on taking the shortest route possible by the birds. Without thinking they poured some water on his head, in spite of the drizzle. No response. They cleaned away the blood that was still oozing from his head, cleared his wounds and bandaged the open cut. But he still did not respond.

"Oh my God!" cried Trixy, tears rolling down her face. "Is he dead?"

"No, not yet. But he will soon be, if we cannot get him to a doctor immediately." Raja looked very demoralised as he stood there, fighting to hold back his tears.

Kharga didn't say anything. He simply picked up Cocky in his arms and set him down under the shade of a large tree. He then cupped his hands and gave a call. Soon a couple of lizards slithered up to them. They were green and long and quite uncommon in this region, which generally saw the colourless ones lazing in the sun, on the rocks.

Raja promptly jumped back in fright, as the one thing he couldn't stand was the sight of a lizard. Obviously there was some communication between the boy and the lizards, as they suddenly darted away as quickly as they had appeared. Not much later they returned, with

something clutched in their tiny jaws. They were leaves of some kind. Kharga rubbed the leaves hard against his palms to dry them. He then cut them and squeezed the juice on to Cocky's wounds. After covering the open wounds with the milky juice, he placed a large leaf over it and once again bandaged the area. The bleeding stopped soon, and five minutes later Cocky revived.

*****

When I opened my eyes I saw a white flash and felt a searing pain through my head. I shut my eyes and tried to get used to the pain. When it eased off to an extent, I opened my eyes slowly. Three extremely worried faces were looking down at me. I was under a tree and it had stopped raining.

*"He's alright!"* screamed a delighted Trixy as I groaned. She impulsively licked my face and head.

"Stop it!!" shouted Raja. "What are you trying to do, drown him?"

When the welcome was over and I could stand groggily on my feet, I informed them of my misadventure.

"And these are the lizards that found the special leaves that cured you," informed Trixy. "Kharga says only they know where such leaves are found."

I was about to thank them in some way, when suddenly a large eagle swooped down, grabbed one of the lizards in its talons, and flew away. At once the other lizard scampered away for cover. Aghast, I asked Kharga accusingly, "You could have stopped that eagle! Why didn't you?"

He looked pensive but not guilty. "That's nature. One shouldn't meddle with nature."

There was a short pause. "The poacher's hideout must be in these parts," mulled Kharga, trying to change the topic. "So they could be holed up close by..."

"HEY!! What are you...?" someone called out aloud. It was the man I had followed and he was climbing back towards the town. "...Er, aren't you Kharga Bahadur?"

I informed the others about him. Raja immediately started growling, and menacingly stepped towards the man. The man looked at me, recognition registering in his eyes, and looked back at Kharga in amazement. Fretting, he stepped back from the advancing Raja, turned on his heels and ran back the way he had come.

"He's on to us," I warned the others. "He has realised what we are here for and must have gone back to call the others, and probably relocate the skins."

"Let's call the police," suggested Kharga, looking out of depth in such a situation.

"But that will give them ample time to take what they want and disappear," Raja, the practical thinker, opined. "No, we need to get them now on our own, or we'll have lost an opportunity."

"But if he spots us following him he might mislead us."

"Let him go," Trixy stepped forward. "Give him five more minutes, and we can go after them. With his fresh scent and no more rains, I can easily follow his trail."

So we waited for five minutes and Trixy's sensitive nose, that had helped us on an earlier occasion, took over. She followed his scent as confidently as if he were just five feet away. But in the five minutes of reprieve he received, I got some very special attention from Trixy, and, expectedly, disapproving looks from Raja. Must remember to knock and injure myself, the next time we have a fight.

It was just as well we didn't waste any further time because, as Trixy led us to a small hamlet, we saw two men scampering away. They were carrying a well-covered bundle each, and were about to enter a glade. One of them was Jeetu, the man I had followed.

To cut the short story shorter still, while Raja, Trixy and I chased the men and basically bothered them, Kharga Bahadur warned the hamlet and returned with three able-bodied men. Both the villains were captured and the skins recovered. We marched them off to the nearest police station and let the three men there take credit for the dramatic capture of the poachers, along with full information of their accomplices.

"Great!" cried Raja happily, in spite of Trixy trotting right next to him. "That made me feel good... and hungry."

"What happens now?" I asked Kharga Bahadur. "Do you resume your rescue missions?"

"I am not sure," he said sadly. "Maybe they are safer there in their cages. Maybe, in a strange way, this is nature too."

❑❑❑

# 4

# Two Buttons and a Pin

It was almost 9 o'clock and Rishi was sure he'd be late for school. His father's car had once again conked out at the last minute and he had 15 minutes to cover the two kilometres to school. Thanks to the heavy backpack it took him ten minutes of a half-jog, half-run to cover the first kilometre. Now he was running at full pace, and as he turned at the corner of Jaggu Modi's shop, there was a mighty collision. Next instant he was on the ground lying on his back, looking up at the bright blue skies, and the face of a very frightened boy.

"S... sorry!" the boy said, jumping away from Rishi. He frantically looked around the corner where he had come from. He heard footsteps of someone running. Confusion and desperation written all over his face, the boy tried to decide which way to go.

"Jump over the containers and hide behind the counter," said Rishi impulsively, pointing to Jaggu Modi's shop. The boy hesitated, but just for a moment, and then like an athlete he gingerly stepped over the tin containers with rice and dals, and sprang over the counter.

"WHAT THE..." Jaggu Modi shouted, getting to his feet.

"It's okay, Jaggu mama, he is my friend. Please let him hide," cried Rishi, getting off the ground. Before Jaggu could protest, two burly policemen charged around the corner and stood before them, panting.

"Did you... did you... see a boy... running this way?" asked one of them, clearly out of breath.

"He went into that lane," said Rishi glibly, pointing to a narrow road.

"Let's go," puffed the heavier policemen, and the two trudged on.

After they were out of sight, Jaggu found his voice. "Now look here Rishi, that was not a clever thing to do, helping a criminal."

"But I am not a criminal," protested the boy, slowly peering over the counter. He checked to see if the coast was clear and jumped back onto the road. Rishi saw he was more-or-less his own age, with large, bright eyes and a shock of black, curly hair. He was very poorly dressed, in almost a uniform, and extremely skinny.

He stretched out his hand hesitatingly to Rishi, "Thank you, friend."

Rishi took his hand automatically. "Why were they chasing you? What did you do?"

"It's a long story," he said apologetically. "But I've got to go."

"Wait! You don't look well. Would you like to eat something?"

That stopped him. He looked longingly at Rishi but suddenly decided, "No, thank you. I must get away from..."

"Please!" Rishi himself couldn't understand why he was going out of his way to help this boy. "There's a tea-shop just around this corner." He didn't wait for an answer. He held the boy by his wrist and guided him to the tea-shop. The chimes of a clock told him it was 9 o'clock already, and that meant trouble at school. But an unspoken voice told him this was more important.

Without a word the boy went through two plates of idlis and another two plates of dosas. Rishi sat back, and watched him silently. Only after the boy had finished, he asked, "What's your name?"

"Dhanu."

"I've never seen you before."

"I'm not from this town. I'm from Maiti village."

"What happened? You don't look like a criminal to me, so why were the police chasing you?"

Dhanu pondered awhile, as though considering where to start. "A year ago," he finally began, "I was with some of my friends and we were visiting a village one of my friends came from. After a meal at his house, he took us to some other friend's house. Suddenly a warning came, 'Run! Police!!' A few packets of white powder were thrown away and everyone tried to escape. I was the only one caught. The packets turned out to be drugs and I was accused of dealing in it. Till that day, I had not even seen drugs.

"I was convicted and sent off to a rehabilitation centre, a kind of correction house for wayward boys. It was horrible. The place was horrible, the people that managed the place were treacherous, and most of the boys, the inmates, were criminals, or criminally inclined. I escaped twice from that place and twice I was caught. Each time my punishment was harsher.

"I knew that if left in that place, and with such company, I too would perhaps become criminally inclined. Believe me, there was no way of escaping that fate if I remained there. If I wanted to maintain my sanity and remain normal, I had to get out of that system. So when they were transferring me two days ago to a more lethal and inescapable house, I made the most of my chance and escaped en route. I've been on the run for 48 hours and here I am."

It was the most tragic story Rishi had ever heard. "Wh... what about your parents, your family?"

"They didn't believe me either... and disowned me."

"Good God!! Whatever will you do now? The police will eventually catch you... and you may get deeper in trouble."

For an answer Dhanu put his head in his arms and wept.

*****

By now, Rishi had given up the idea of attending school for the day. He felt he simply must do something for this boy. They were still out in the streets and walking towards Rishi's home. He had no idea where he was going to put him up or what he would do with him. He doubted if his parents would allow Dhanu to stay at their place, but if he were left on the streets, it would be a matter of time before he was caught.

"The clothes you are wearing will surely give you away," he said, observing the khaki shirt and half-pant Dhanu was wearing. "I'll give you some of mine... though they may be a little loose for you. What else do you have on you?"

Dhanu fiddled in both pockets as though searching for something, and when he pulled his fists out they held two buttons and a pin. "They came off when the police tried to grab me," he explained.

That will not take him far either, thought Rishi.

They reached Rishi's house, a small row house in a short street of row houses, and still he was undecided about what he would do. But seeing the garage, with the car still in it, gave him an idea. "Father's car is not running. Knowing him, it will remain unattended for a few days. The garage will be the perfect place for you to hide, till at least we decide on our next move."

The garage was fairly large with sufficient space to move around. "I'll just shut the door, not bolt it, and you can sleep in the backseat of the car. Believe me it's the safest place for you."

*****

Rishi hated doing it but he had to lie to his mother for not attending school. "I felt dizzy and my tummy ached and..." He was going to lay it a bit thicker but his mother stopped him.

"No lunch or dinner for you," came her all-too-familiar remedy. Rishi feared the next part of her therapy even more. A large peg of castor oil! He didn't know who invented that poison, but he was sure he must have burnt in hell a thousand times a day, with curses from children all over the world. The taste of that liquid was bound to make a person ill, true and proper.

After the second part of the therapy took its course, Rishi seriously wondered if he did the right thing for Dhanu, and whether he was worth so much trouble.

In fact, what drew Rishi's mind and heart was the mental trauma Dhanu must have gone through. First to be falsely accused of a crime, then to share a place with the scum of the earth, be ill treated, go hungry, disturb one's education... and finally, the cruellest blow of all... his own parents not believing him. Dhanu suffered all this for an entire year. Rishi wondered if he could live through such trauma for even a day. Parents' love and respect was one of the most precious gifts to a child. Another lesson he learnt from this experience – be very careful in selecting friends. In the end, he concluded, this boy needed a friend, and he would be that friend.

Smuggling out lunch for Dhanu presented no problem. In fact the two shared the lunch equally as Rishi too was hungry, the castor oil already compelling him to visit the bathroom thrice in the last one hour.

*****

The first problem arose when Rakhi, Rishi's younger sister, came back from school. She dumped her bags and announced, "I'm going cycling with my friends." Her small bicycle was parked in the garage.

Rishi raced to beat her to the door of the garage. If she came to know of Dhanu, the rest of the town would come to know of it inside five minutes, he knew. Then speaking louder than usual, he told her, "I'll get your cycle. It's very dirty inside today after father could not start the car." That should make Dhanu take cover, thought Rishi.

"Okay," she said, puzzled. "But why are you shouting?"

He tried shutting the door behind him as he went inside the garage, but she opened it wide. He removed the cover of the cycle, and saw Dhanu crouching behind it. He quickly threw the cover over him and wheeled the cycle out.

"Why did you throw the cover on the ground?" Rakhi questioned. "You know I leave it on the hook."

"I know, I know," he said impatiently. "I'll do just that. Now go!" She looked at him enquiringly. "And when you return," he called out to her as she mounted the cycle, "let me know. I'll keep it back inside."

With a sigh of relief, Rishi went back inside the garage to chat with Dhanu.

"I think the best option for you would be to leave this town," he suggested. "The police know you are here and will keep looking for you."

"But where could I go? If I go back to my own village, I'll be caught there too and handed over to the police."

"I was thinking of a town called Davakottai. My mother's parents stay there. If I write them a note saying you are my friend, I am sure they'll help out. And the police there won't be..."

A commotion had broken outside. "It's Major Nair's voice. He is our neighbour... a very hot-tempered man."

Rishi stepped out and saw what he hated to see... violence. Major Nair, a retired army officer, was holding his servant Bablu by the collar and slapping him hard. Rishi had often chatted with Bablu and found him a pleasant enough fellow.

"Thief!! *Namak haram!!*" the Major yelled, and with each abuse he smacked the young man. Rishi tried to stop the beating by jumping over the fence and running between the two. But in the process, he took a blow himself. As he went off-balance, the Major's attention was drawn towards him. In the split second afforded, Bablu wrenched himself free and ran away.

"Now look what you've done, you meddling little..." the Major angrily voiced his opinion at Rishi's interference. Nobody in the neighbourhood particularly liked the

Major, but they all respected him. He was an honourable man, quite rich and lived alone.

Rishi's mother came rushing and the Major quietened down. "What happened?" she asked.

"I caught Bablu stealing, red-handed," said the Major, red with excitement, "and was taking him to the police when your son interfered and now he has run away."

"That's too bad, but I suppose your brother and his team will catch him again," Rishi's mother reminded him. The Major's brother was the Chief Inspector of the local police.

It took a good hour for things to settle down. The police were called, details given, and promises made. When it was all over, Rishi returned to his own home. He saw Rakhi outside the garage and panicked.

"When did you get back?"

"Ten minutes ago. Why?"

"Where's your bike?"

"Inside the garage, and it's not as dirty as you claimed."

Rishi gulped hard. "And...?"

"And tomorrow is a holiday, so I'll be going out with my friends on the bike again. You can take it out at ten o'clock."

Normally Rishi would have given her a rap on the back of her head for being so impudent. But today he just replied numbly, "Sure." How she didn't spot Dhanu, he didn't know. But some good luck must stick with that boy sometimes, he thought.

*****

The night was not restful for Rishi as he tossed and turned from one side of the bed to the other. The day's happenings were playing in his mind as though he had pressed the rewind button of his video and was now replaying all the incidents. To make matters worse, the castor oil had taken full effect and his empty stomach continuously grumbled about being victimised. He could not even risk taking food out for Dhanu.

When finally sleep did come, he was rudely awakened by a crashing sound. Even as he tried to figure out where the sound came from, he heard shouts of: *"HELP!! Murderer!!"*

It was Major Nair's voice again.

Lights came jumping to life as every nearby house was suddenly alight. By the time the Subramanium family ran out, a small crowd had already assembled in the garden of Major Nair's house. In the middle of the crowd was the Major, spread-eagled over a boy's body. It was Dhanu. Lying next to his outstretched hand was a knife.

"Well done Major Saab, you got him well and proper," said someone from the crowd.

"You betcha!" cried the Major, obviously proud of himself. "The knife proves he could be a killer." He got up maintaining a strong grip on his victim.

"How could Dhanu do this?" Rishi asked himself miserably. "How could he so callously let down my trust in him? And to think all day I was helping a hardcore criminal."

"But it's only a boy," said Manu Subramanium, Rishi's father.

"Boys can kill too." The Major dragged the boy towards his door.

*"But I was only trying to help!"* screamed Dhanu, looking directly at Rishi and realising he did not believe him either. "There was this man sneaking into the house. I tried to catch him. He was holding that knife... he chased me... until I fell into that window and broke the glass. That scared him and he ran away."

"A likely story," sneered the Major. "So where is this man?"

"He ran away! I think he was coming to kill you!"

Dhanu caught Rishi's eye again, imploring him to believe his words. But what could Rishi do? He wanted to believe him. He had believed him earlier, but now...? Yet, seeing Dhanu's earnest and sincere face, he once again mellowed. This cannot be the face of a killer.

"Please father, tell the Major not to hurt him," he implored his father. Manu was puzzled by the request. But knowing his son's abhorrence of violence, he tried to bring down tempers.

"Let's not take any hasty action," he cried out aloud, holding back the Major's hand, which was about to strike Dhanu. "The police will be here any minute, they'll take proper steps."

"There is only one proper step for such boys," shouted the Major, annoyed at being made to stop from taking any action, "and that is the taste of a thrashing!"

Soon the police came and took charge of Dhanu. As they escorted him to their jeep, he kept looking towards Rishi. A minute later, he was gone. The Major was to submit his complaint at the Police Station the next day.

What a nightmare, thought Rishi, as he joined his family back home. Here he was trying to help Dhanu, and instead, Dhanu was in deeper trouble now than he was before. An armed burglary accusation would surely put him away for a few years.

But could Dhanu have done such a thing? After all Rishi didn't know him that well, considering he met him for the first time just that morning. Could he be telling the truth? Was that really not his knife?

Suddenly he remembered he had checked Dhanu's pockets earlier in the day. All he had were the two buttons and a pin. So that certainly couldn't be his knife. It certainly was not a knife from the garage either, as he would have recognised it. And if the knife was not his, as Dhanu claimed, then the rest of his story could possibly be true too. Was he, once again, being misjudged? That would be a double tragedy, and he certainly would not allow that to happen, promised Rishi determinedly. He would give Dhanu the benefit of doubt, once again.

*****

Next morning, a Sunday, Rishi went to the garage to investigate if Dhanu had left a clue behind. He went through it half a dozen times, but found nothing.

"Okay, you can bring it out now! I'm here!" He heard Rakhi call out.

"What?"

"My cycle. You told me yesterday you'll bring it out."

"Come and fetch it yourself," was the angry retort from Rishi.

"I've known you all my life, but I still don't understand you," grumbled Rakhi, entering the garage and wheeling her cycle out.

Rishi hunted some more for clues but finally gave up. "Wish I could have spoken to him even for a minute. Maybe he..."

A booming voice outside made him step out. "Good morning, good morning! A very good morning!" The Major was dressed in his military best, complete with a scarf, baton and all. His face was beaming and there was an added military gait to his steps. "Wonderful morning, isn't it?"

"Yes," agreed Manu Subramanium, joining the Major in the garden, "it's a Sunday." Rishi's father worked very hard all week, so Sunday to him was like candy to a child... to be enjoyed thoroughly. "But where are you off to?"

"Have you forgotten? Today I have to give my Firsthand Information Report at the Police Station... two cases, including Bablu's attempted burglary. And I'll do it with pleasure, just to keep such ruffians off the road."

Police Station? This was Rishi's chance to meet Dhanu.

"Can I go along too?"

"What?? I'm going to the Police Station young man, not to a movie! What business would you have there?"

"Nothing, except to gain some experience on the functioning of a Police Station, just as I'd like to see the inside of a military base."

"Hmmmm! Good, good. Always good to see young men with interests. Okay, hop along, if it's fine with your father."

It was fine with him, so shortly the two were at the door of the Police Station. "No monkey business from you now. Remember you are at a Police Station, and my brother is very strict."

As the Major went through the formalities, Dhanu was brought in their presence for identification. Rishi was overwhelmed with sadness when he saw him. His hands were tied with a rope as thick as his limbs, and he wore the most desolate and dejected expression on his face. His eyes lit up upon spotting Rishi, but only for a brief second.

"We are obliged to you for catching this little rascal, brother," the inspector was saying. "We were hunting for him for the last three days after he escaped from a nearby rehabilitation centre."

Dhanu and his escort were standing right next to Rishi. He took the risk and whispered, "I believe you, Dhanu."

Instantly a smile crept on Dhanu's face. It was almost as if a heavy load had been lifted off his head.

"What did he look like?" Rishi tried speaking as softly as possible. "Any way I can recognise him?"

Dhanu checked to see if anyone was overhearing them. But the others were busy with their own work and his escort had stepped forward to the inspector's table to sign a document.

"I am not sure... it was dark. He was about 16–17 years old, a little on the heavy side and he called me a 'boka'. He also looked somewhat familiar, but I just can't..."

"What are you two whispering?" called out the inspector loudly, and Rishi's private interrogation ceased.

*****

Later, after reaching home, Rishi tried to piece together the information he had received and find out if it could help in determining the real culprit. It didn't. There were hundreds, if not thousands, of 16 to 17-year-olds who were a little on the heavier side in the town itself. It would be impossible to check them out. Dhanu said he found him familiar, but Rishi did not know anyone Dhanu would know. And the word 'boka' – he had no idea what it meant. It was not a Tamil word and didn't even sound Hindi. But then, he reasoned, if it was not a common word, its origin would certainly narrow the flied of suspects. So, he decided, his focus should be on finding the word's meaning, or at least its place of origin.

"Never heard of it," was the response from his father, when he put forward the question at lunchtime. It was the same answer he received from the rest of the family and friends. He had even got in touch with the three hotels in town, as hotels generally housed people from other cities and states. He met a Punjabi, a Gujarati and a Bihari, but none knew the word. By teatime he had given up. Maybe there was no such word, Rishi reasoned unhappily. Maybe...

The telephone rang. It was his mother's sister from Kolkata. It was a ritual between the two sisters to get in touch every Sunday afternoon.

"Mum," Rishi called out to his mother who was upstairs. "Sheela masi for you!"

"Coming," he heard her. That meant he had to keep the conversation going for at least two minutes.

"Masi, have you ever heard of the word 'boka'?" Rishi asked casually.

"WHAT?? Where in heavens did you hear that word," Sheela masi asked incredulously.

"It... it just cropped up. Have you heard it?"

"Yes, but it's not a word I would like my nephew to use."

Success!! "Is it a Bengali word? What does it mean?"

"Well, if you must know, yes it is a Bengali slang word, and it means... kind of stupid... or mad... But don't you ever use it. Now where is my lazy sister?"

A Bengali slang word? Who would use a Bengali slang word in Pudukkotai, this small town of Tamil Nadu? There hardly were any Bengalis here, and...

"BABLU!!" he called out aloud. Bablu, Major Nair's servant, was a Bengali from Murshidabad in West Bengal. Rishi had never heard him use that word before during their occasional meetings. But as his aunt had pointed out, it was a derogatory word, and probably Bablu was careful not to use it loosely. "And yes," his thought process continued, "he should have been our first suspect after what had happened the morning before. He had probably come to take revenge on the Major for thrashing him."

And Dhanu had found the attacker familiar! But Rishi was sure Dhanu had not set eyes on Bablu before. Not even on the first day, when the Major beat up Bablu, as Dhanu was then hiding in the garage. So how was he familiar with Bablu?

Besides this, all the rest sounded just right. But what should be his next move. The ideal thing would be for Bablu to confess, but that seemed hardly likely. How could one make him come forward and admit that he was the guilty party... if he was the guilty party?

The first thing to do was to find Bablu. Rishi knew where he lived, on the fringes of the town. But the police knew that too and they must have already looked for him there. No, he must have gone into hiding and would remain out of sight. He may already have left town.

Till early evening, Rishi mused over the problem until an idea hit him finally. Chandu, Bablu's friend, was the answer.

*****

"I don't like this at all!" Manu Subramanium told his son angrily. "I can't believe I am spending my Sunday night like this."

"You're complaining? What about me?" Manu's friend, Anthony, complained. "There I was clad in my comfortable lungi, sitting in my favourite armchair and watching an exciting one-day match. And then you call me for this... this... vigilance."

Manu, Anthony and Rishi were all in Manu's garage. No place to sit, no lights and very hot. It was past eleven in the night, and they were already there for over an hour.

"What makes you so sure Bablu will come?"

"I am not so sure, father. But if my reading is correct, he should be here."

"Frankly, I have no idea how you came to the conclusion that it was Bablu who intended to harm old Major Nair, and not that boy in the prison."

"Trust me, father. Another few hours and we'll know."

"What I want to know is why haven't you at least arranged for a couple of chairs?" asked an irritated Anthony. "Come, let's sit in the car."

"It's very, very hot in there," warned Manu, himself sweating heavily and regretting calling his friend after his son had suggested an additional hand.

"You mean, you haven't yet put an AC in it?" Anthony asked incredulously.

"An AC in this car? Huh! With the weight of an AC it will not move an inch."

"It's not moving an inch in any case."

"Will you two please stop fighting? Even if Bablu does come, you'll certainly scare him away. And we want to catch him, not scare him away."

The two friends grumbled but kept quiet. Anthony slid to the ground and sat down, back to the car. Soon Manu followed suit, and a little later both started snoring lightly.

Rishi stood by the door, keeping a constant watch on his neighbour's little garden. "Hope Bablu falls for my bait," he worried, "or these two will never let me forget it. And poor Dhanu... God only knows whatever will happen to him."

As the clock in the house struck 12, he too began feeling drowsy. He wished he could sit down awhile, but that might make him sleepier, and the entire plot could backfire if Bablu reached the Major unnoticed. He wanted to inform the Major of his plot too, but he felt the man would probably ruin everything with his attitude.

It was not very dark outside, thanks to the streetlights, and Rishi was sure he would be able to spot Bablu if he tried to cross the garden. With the help of his father and Anthony, he was certain they would be able to overpower Bablu.

The clock struck one and still everything was quiet. The snoring of his two senior companions soon became louder and more rhythmic. Rishi's eyes were half closed, when he heard the click of a door shutting. He jumped to attention. There was still no one in the garden. And then he saw a movement behind the curtain, on the ground floor window of the Major's house.

"Quick!!" Rishi awakened Manu and Anthony. "He's already in!"

The three charged out of the garage, jumped over the connecting fence (which Anthony managed on the fifth attempt) and rushed to the door. It was locked.

"Move aside!" ordered the burly Anthony. He took two steps back and crashed into the door, breaking open the latch. They rushed in. In the dim shadows they saw someone about to go up the stairs, and all three sprang on the figure and brought him down.

*"HELP!! HELP!!"* cried aloud the man under them. "MURDERERS!! LOOTERS!!" the voice carried on. Rishi switched on the lights and regretted ever being born. The man they had caught was the Major himself.

"Wh... what are you doing here?" asked Manu, quickly getting off the Major.

"What do you mean, you nincompoop!! I live here, remember? I came down just to get a glass of water, and the whole damn army jumps on me!!"

It took a good 15 minutes and a thousand apologies to calm down the old Major. But eventually, the three did manage to leave the house with severe warnings that the father and son team should never darken his doorsteps again, and that the fat hoodlum who broke down his door must repair it by 10 a.m. the next morning.

Further vigilance was cancelled with immediate effect, with Anthony promising Manu that he would never forgive him for this night. And a bleary-eyed Manu promising Rishi, "We'll discuss this first thing in the morning." Rishi's fervent appeals to continue the watch fell on deaf ears and dead minds, as both the seniors made their way via the shortest route to bed. Rishi alone manned his post at the garage once again.

*****

It was two in the morning and peace and quiet had returned to the small street of row houses, except for an occasional snort and an angry, 'Blast them', call from the Major's window. How he was going to keep awake next day at school Rishi had no idea and soon he was consumed with drowsiness and fatigue.

The clock struck three and Rishi's eyes snapped open. He had once again dozed off. Maybe a walk would help keep him awake. He stretched, rubbed his eyes and stepped out. It was much cooler and the soft breeze revived his sagging spirits. He took in a few large gulps of the fresh air and was about to return to the garage when he saw a figure walking down the street. It wasn't a common sight, not at three in the morning, figured Rishi. He quickly ducked behind the fence.

The figure stopped in front of the Major's house. It was Bablu. With the deftness of a cat he leapt over the garden gate and in a few quick steps was at the door of the house.

Oh no, worried Rishi. The door was broken. Sure enough, in a moment Bablu was inside the house. Rishi desperately wondered what he should do. If he raised the alarm, Bablu would once again run away and escape. If he tried to tackle him alone, Bablu would easily overpower him. If he kept silent, Bablu would kill the Major. But he was taking too much time thinking. He must do something NOW.

He quickly jumped the connecting fence, picked up a small pebble and threw it through the Major's bedroom window upstairs, praying it would fall on him and rouse him from his sleep. There was a soft clatter upstairs and he realised he had missed his target. He too went to the door and entered the house. He could at least try and stop Bablu from escaping.

As his eyes adjusted to the darkness inside, Rishi headed for the staircase, intending to follow Bablu. Suddenly, he stopped dead in his tracks. Halfway up the stairs was Bablu, looking down directly at him. The two maintained their positions without moving, without speaking.

Finally, Rishi said, "Give yourself up, Bablu. What you've done till now is nothing as serious as what you've come to do."

A brief silence followed. "Is that you, Rishi?"

"Yes."

"Go back home, Rishi. I don't want to harm you."

"You don't want to harm the old Major, either."

"That man deserves it. He humiliated me in front of everyone. You saved me that day by interfering. I'm letting you go for that."

"I am not going, Bablu. You know an innocent boy is being blamed for your action."

"I know that," he said with a short laugh. "That boy has a knack of getting into trouble. Do you know that's the second time he has showed up when he shouldn't have? And both the times he's paid for the mistake."

"How?"

"I remembered him from an earlier incident, about a year ago. He, with his friends, was visiting a colleague of mine. The police came suddenly and we all escaped, but that boy got caught... with our consignment of drugs. Poor fellow could not prove his innocence and ha, ha, ha, the police got off our backs. After that incident I came over to this village and worked in this house."

Rishi was aghast at the cruel chain of events that had totally ruined the life of an innocent boy. "You are still young, Bablu. Give yourself up. You'll get a lighter sentence and you will be saving a boy."

"Ha, ha, ha! Are you kidding? As far as I am concerned, he was expendable. And so are you, my dear friend. You know too much. Now I'll have to kill you first, and then the Major." With that he came threateningly towards Rishi, knife held in front of him.

Suddenly lights flooded the room. "No one is going to kill anyone!" It was the Major. He was standing on the landing upstairs, a cocked gun in his hands.

*****

Rishi's warning pebble had woken up the Major and he had heard the entire exchange of words between Bablu and himself. They took Bablu to the Police Station that very night and upon the Major's word got Dhanu released.

"But what I don't understand," the Major was saying as he drove the two boys back home, "is how you were so sure Bablu would come today."

"Last evening I had informed his best friend Chandu that you had found certain evidence against Bablu that would certainly put him behind bars. And you would hand over that evidence to the police in the morning. As that didn't seem to bother Chandu much, I added that if Bablu got caught he would also implicate Chandu, since he had often talked to me about his bad habits. I was hoping he would pass on this message to Bablu, which he obviously did."

"Whew! You took some chances, particularly on my life, didn't you?"

"Maybe," replied Rishi dolefully.

"But I am more worried about Dhanu. What will he do now? Though his name has been cleared, he says he won't go back to his village."

Dhanu sat alone at the back. The same thought was going through his own mind. Maybe if he found work here...

The Major interrupted Rishi's thoughts. "Remember, Dhanu came to help me, when he saw Bablu. At great risk to his own life, he tackled that killer. Such acts of bravery never go unrewarded in the Indian Army, and it will not go unrewarded by me either. From now on, I will be his Godfather. I'll see to it that he continues with his education. He can stay with me. I believe I need some young company."

As dawn broke and the skies lightened, so did the boys' spirits. Both knew it was going to be a bright and beautiful day. There was justice in this world, after all. It may be delayed, but eventually, justice is done. No words were spoken but both knew a deep bond had been formed... far, far stronger than words could describe.

# 5

# Two Hours of Doom

It was a month since Shiv had visited Nizams, the famous *kathi rolls* restaurant in Central Kolkata. Ever since his strange adventure in the land of the Tenkos, he was apprehensive of visiting Nizams... at least the extraordinary 'cabin' which was the doorway to different dimensions and different times of this world. Not that he had not enjoyed his 'five minutes' in Tenko land... Far from it, it was the best time he had had till date. He had achieved self-esteem at the end of the adventure. Something he never knew before. So, he was all but itching for another adventure and, of course, not to forget his prime motive for visiting Nizams... the delicious *kathi rolls*.

But yes, ever since he had returned from that adventure, something was nagging him. Was it okay to use that doorway? It certainly was not natural to meddle with time and dimensions. What if he got caught in a different dimension, as he almost did, or in a different time period, and couldn't return to AD 2004, Kolkata, India? What if some monster devoured him for dinner, as one almost did in his last adventure? What would his family do, with absolutely no clue of finding out what happened to him? For, he had certainly never talked to anyone about his recent adventure. These thoughts bothered him and with great will power he kept away from Nizams. Yet, the craving for adventure and the hunger for another juicy *kathi roll* can together overwhelm any flimsy negative thought.

"There you are! I was sure you would return soon, though you did take your time." It was the old man guarding his 'cabin'. His milky white beard was well groomed as usual. Shiv hesitated. He was still not sure if he had come to the restaurant just for the rolls or... He smiled at the old man, but sat down in the main hall, some distance away from him.

"It's no use avoiding it," said the old man with a confident laugh. "Once you've been through it, you will never want to stop coming."

Shiv pretended not to pay attention and called for his favourite, two *double-chicken-unda kathi rolls*. The old man stood firm where he was, eyes twinkling in quiet mirth, forefinger twirling his beard. The rolls came and, with a determined effort, Shiv concentrated on enjoying them. Finishing his meal, he made his way to the exit without looking at the old man and the cabin. At the doorway he stopped. There really was no need to be rude to the old man, he thought. He turned around and walked back to him.

"I wanted to thank you for the last time. It was great."

"I know," the old man said non-committally.

Shiv glanced at the special cabin. It was an old wooden cabin and at the head of the entrance was the legendary number 8. Not a lucky number by Vaastu. It was almost illegible, as it was coated with the varnish used on the wooden framework itself.

"Er... just for my information... where else does the cabin take you?"

"Anywhere, any time."

"And by 'time' you mean... in the past, or in the future?"

"Both. Where do you want to go?"

"No, no!" Shiv said quickly. "I just wanted to know."

"Of course."

"Thank you then, I'll be pushing on." Shiv turned to go.

"Bye-bye."

Shiv turned back to him. "By the way, how much in the future can I go?"

"As far ahead as you want. But each of our day is reserved for one particular period."

"Gosh!" Shiv's eyes lit up. "What period is on for today?"

"The 35$^{th}$ century!"

"Good God!" Shiv exclaimed, visualising the modern wonders he'd be able to witness. "Fifteen hundred years from now?"

"About. Want to go?"

"Not really... but... how long before I can come back?"

"An hour... a day... a year... a century, anything!"

"An hour! I'd like to try an hour," he submitted, both with eager anticipation and cautiousness too. He checked his watch and corrected himself, "Make it two hours. I have that much time in hand before I'm due to return home."

*****

Shiv entered the cabin with the swing doors. The instant the old man shut the swing doors, Shiv heard the same loud bang and saw the blinding light. He immediately covered his eyes. When he opened them again, he was prepared to witness a most amazing place, a place nobody on earth in the 21st century could have imagined... a place replete with advanced technology, science and ultramodern visions.

Holding his breath, he stepped out of a rusty metal enclosure he had landed in. It was the doorway on the other side of the 'magical connection'. His first sight was of an extremely tall and slim man standing at the entrance. And unbelievably, he had oriental looks. He was obviously the keeper of the connection at this end.

"Welcome," the tall man said, bowing low. "I am Slim Chang, and you are my first guest ever."

'Slim', Shiv could understand. But what was a 'Chang' doing here in Kolkata? There were Chinese in Kolkata in the 21st century, but the way their numbers were reducing Shiv was sure there wouldn't be any left by the 22nd century.

He threw a quick glance around him. He was near a mid-sized town. The houses were not much different, the streets were wide but there were very few people on the road. And whoever was on the road was oriental. This puzzled him. He had travelled just in time, so where he stood now was exactly on the same grounds as where he had started off from... Nizams. Of course, there was no Nizams any longer, he could accept that, tough though it was, but he should have still been in central Kolkata, in West Bengal, which was in dear India. As such he had expected a traditional Bengali welcome.

"Hello," said Shiv, giving a curt bow. "I am Shiv Sen." He once again looked around him in amazement, but just couldn't come to terms with what he saw. "Tell me Slim, where am I?"

"China!" said Slim, showing all his 32 well-formed teeth.

"China? But I thought I had simply travelled in time. So logically, I should still be in Kolkata."

"Kolkata? Where's that?"

"In India, of course. That's where I come from, you know. So how come I am in China now?"

"Because now the whole world is China," Slim explained, smiling even more broadly and showing two more teeth Shiv had not noticed earlier.

Shiv heard him and understood what he said. But he was equally sure that what he understood and what was just said must be two different things. "No, no, no!" he said, trying to simplify matters. "The whole world has two hundred-plus countries. Of course, China is one of them but there are others like India, USA, Pakistan... is Pakistan still there?"

"No, no, no!" Slim mimicked Shiv. "Now there is only one country in the world... China."

Shiv was sure Slim couldn't smile any wider, but that's exactly what he did as he spoke.

"But... but what happened to the other countries?" Shiv asked incredulously.

"Gone!" Now Shiv was sure this man's face was going to crack in two as he stretched his smile to an unimaginable length. Before Shiv could ask 'Where?' Slim clarified, "Wars! Terrorism! Epidemics! For five hundred years these three curses, but mainly the first two, reduced the original world by half. By the year AD 2500, the population of the rest of the world was half of China's. By the year 3000 they were ten per cent of our population. So we took over."

When the truth finally dawned on Shiv he almost collapsed to the ground. "You... you mean... there are no more Indians? No more Bengalis?"

"Well, technically, no!" The smile had become stagnant, now that it had reached its absolute limit.

What a calamity, thought Shiv. No one in the 21st century would have imagined what our world was heading towards.

"But you? China? How did you escape being wiped out?"

"Simple! We didn't fight!"

Shiv desperately wished he could wipe that ridiculous smile off Slim's face. It was interfering with his thought process. He thought he had had enough of Slim, and needed to look around and talk with other people, before he returned home. He checked his watch. He had already wasted ten minutes.

"I'll just walk around and see things for myself," he said.

"Sure, but don't go too far. Your return slot is 1 hour 50 minutes away. You miss that and you'll have to remain here till another 'delivery' arrives, which may be a few hundred years from now."

"You can count on your smile I'll be back before that," Shiv promised and hurried away. Under no circumstances whatsoever was he going to be late for this appointment.

For the first time Shiv had the opportunity to study where he was. The small town he had seen was more or less the same, as it had existed in the 21st century. Where were the mammoth skyscrapers, the zooming vehicles, the billions of inhabitants he had expected to see? With great trepidation he proceeded up a small road. As one of Shiv's legs was shorter than the other, he walked with a pronounced limp.

He could see quite a few workers in the distance, all working in a paddy field. He took heart upon seeing their skin colour. They were all brown... definitely Indians. And paddy fields meant, rice. Good, all was not lost, after all.

A little further up he came across a bunch of houses. They too looked a lot like the houses he had left behind in Kolkata. Have they not progressed at all? He saw one or two frightened Indian faces peering at him, careful not to get caught observing. But soon he came across another group of houses, and here the progress was very much in evidence. Here was the full power of modernisation with unimaginable designs and facilities. These were fully occupied and controlled by Chinese.

"Pssst!" somebody hissed from behind Shiv. He turned around and saw an Indian beckoning him from a half-shut window. "Who are you? Have you gone mad? What are you doing outside?" He spoke Bengali, realised a much relieved Shiv.

"I've just come from there," said Shiv, pointing towards the area he had walked from. "I'm from the 21$^{st}$ century."

"*WHAT?*" The man looked aghast. He quickly stepped outside the house, caught Shiv by his hand and pulled him into the house. He looked at Shiv as though he had never seen a human being before. "You know, no one has come here from so far back for at least 200 years. My name is Bhola Nath, and I must say you have appeared at the most inappropriate time."

Shiv wanted to tell him that he didn't drop in; he was invited. Bhola Nath was of medium build, and could easily be overlooked in a crowd of even two people... but for his incredible eyes. They were strong, had great depth and there was no doubt their owner was a leader.

"Tell me Mr Bhola Nath, where are the rest of the Indians? And whatever happened to my India?" blurted Shiv, unable to continue without this information.

"Ssshh... not so loud, or they'll hear you!"

"Who'll hear me? And so what if they hear me?"

"The Chinese. The whole village will be in trouble if they hear such talk. You're from the 21st century, you won't understand what we're going through."

"How did all this happen? What about the rest of the world? Are the other countries living like this too?"

"All are ruled by the Chinese. It all started in 2565, when terrorists from a Middle Eastern country dropped a super-nuclear bomb on the United States of America. More than half of that country was destroyed. They in turn ravaged all of the Middle East with their own bombs. India sided with the United States, so Pakistan dropped a nuclear bomb on Mumbai. All of Western and Central India disappeared. We hit back with everything we had and totally obliterated Pakistan. Billions of people died in that war. It was only sections of Eastern India that survived.

"A few years later, another confrontation took place between Europe and Russia. It was only after they almost annihilated each other that they realised China was behind the provocation. South Eastern countries, along with Japan, fought a long drawn out war with Australia and

New Zealand. Again, no victors. In 2604, all of Africa was afflicted by an unknown disease, which again wiped out almost the whole population. Drugs and revolutions accounted for most of South America.

"Each time a disaster occurred, the Chinese sneaked in through the back door, and took control. During these last few centuries they have simply consolidated their position, bringing the entire world under their rule. They make the natives do the work, while they simply bully. They reap the benefits, while we are made to struggle for survival. They live in unimaginable comfort with every modern luxury, while we live like people from the 5th century... slaves!"

Bhola Nath finished his story and looked at Shiv as though in deep thought. Then he suddenly smiled, as if an idea had hit him. "You know, I'm very happy after all, that you're here today. Come, I want to show you something... something that may give you some hope that all is not lost."

Bhola Nath took Shiv into an inner room, pushed aside a heavy chest of drawers and lifted a trapdoor under it. Below, there was a secret underground chamber. Shiv climbed down behind him and was aghast to see what the large chamber held. There were about 20 armed Indians, and boxes and boxes of arms, ammunition and explosives. The men seemed to be waiting for someone, and looked up in surprise on seeing Shiv. Bhola Nath quickly explained the presence of the stranger. The group hushed into silence and studied Shiv with awe and respect.

"Wh... what's going on here, Bhola Nath?"

"These are bombs and guns and explosives," said a very large man, stepping forward. "We are about to execute the first attack against the Chinese in five hundred years. You have come at a very good time, as we take your presence as auspicious, a good omen. Will you join us?"

"Jo... join you in what?" cried Shiv, shaken up with what he had just heard. "I have no idea what you are talking about!"

"We are a group of about 200 Bengalis," explained Bhola Nath patiently. "Today, with our strike, we begin a revolution. The first of its kind in this part of the world in over five centuries."

Trust the Bengalis to start a revolution, thought Shiv, half with pride, half with apprehension.

*****

Shiv just couldn't believe his ears. "Me in a revolution? What revolution? Against whom? I'm just a boy of ten. I'm not even strong and I have to get back within another hour and a half. And my mother would die of fright if she ever found out I joined a revolution," Shiv rattled off, terrified at the idea of joining a revolution. He pointedly checked his watch. "In fact, I should be leaving right now."

He quickly started climbing up the ladder. Bhola Nath hurried after him. "It's okay, we understand. It was foolish of us to make that suggestion. But please leave this area quickly, as we'll be attacking any minute now."

Bhola Nath helped Shiv get through the trapdoor. As they climbed into the room upstairs, they heard a loud shout outside. Alarmed, Bhola Nath peeped out of the nearest window.

*"Oh my God!!* They've surrounded the house." He ran back into the trapdoor. *"Hurry,* we must get back downstairs. They must have come to know of our revolt."

Before Shiv could react, he was dragged downstairs and the trapdoor secured from below. "*Run friends!! RUN!! They're on to us!!*"

Shiv, in his panicked state of mind, wondered where they would run, as the trapdoor was the only exit. To his utter surprise, the rest of the group scooped up all the arms and ammunition, while Bhola Nath ran up to a wall, turned a hidden lever and pushed hard against it. Like magic, part of the wall shifted inwards. Instantly everyone, including a terribly frightened Shiv, rushed into the opening. That very moment, there came a crashing sound from upstairs.

*"Quick,* close the wall! They'll be here any second."

They hurriedly pushed back the false wall into position. Shiv looked about him. They were in a narrow and low passage... almost like a tunnel. The group quietly and swiftly walked towards the other end of the tunnel. A hundred metres further down the tunnel ended and they all climbed up another staircase. Once upstairs, Shiv noticed they were now in an abandoned house, a hundred metres away from the earlier one.

"We have networked the entire town with our secret tunnels," explained Bhola Nath. "This we believe is our key weapon. We've worked very hard to achieve it... and as hard to keep it a secret."

"Everyone disperse!" ordered Bhola Nath. "We'll meet again in two hours' time at Surojit's house. And then we'll launch our revolution."

Good, thought Shiv. That would be after he returned to the safety of the 21st century. Though, of course, it would be interesting to know the outcome of this struggle.

In ones and twos they all emptied the abandoned house and scampered away in different directions... each with his own share of the arms collected.

"I... I... think I'd better get back to my 'return transport' again, or I may miss it." Shiv looked on all sides wondering which way he should go.

"Yes do that," agreed Bhola Nath, "since this place is going to go up soon. You take that road, going that... *OH NO! They've spotted us.*"

"Who? Where..?"

A loud *'spoosh'* sound came suddenly and the next instant the house next to them dissolved. It seemed to have melted down to nothingness right in front of their eyes... along with a couple of Bhola Nath's men. Shiv realised he had just witnessed the first of the marvels of modern technology. He was not keen any longer to find out more about it.

"RUN LAD, *RUN!!*" Bhola Nath shouted, himself ducking for cover. He did not have to yell, as Shiv needed no prompting. A quick dash and they were behind a house.

"I don't think they saw us running here," panted Bhola Nath, cautiously peeping from the corner of the house.

"Wh... what was that?"

"We call it, the Melter. It's a ray gun that dissolves anything it hits. They generally don't use it, so I suppose they have realised this is no ordinary strike. We better find proper cover before they spot us."

Shiv was right on his heels as they zigged-zagged between covers. They soon reached another house where Bhola Nath knocked frantically. The big man Shiv had seen earlier in the cellar opened it, and they spilled into the house.

"They've got the Melter out, Indrajit," informed Bhola Nath. "Looks like someone has leaked our plans."

"Must be Kalia. He was always after the easy life." The big man had large bushy eyebrows and always looked as though he was about to tear a man apart.

Shiv once again wanted to remind them that he should be leaving. And as he was not part of all this, he was sure the Chinese would let him go. But just seeing the big man and his furious appearance convinced him that now was not the right time. He checked his watch. Just 45 minutes had passed since he had entered the cabin at Nizams. A full hour and 15 minutes to go before he could return. By then, he worried, God only knew what would become of him... a hostage, trapped in another timeframe, or simply burnt to cinders by one of those Melters.

"They will soon find our tunnels and we'll lose our trump card! We've got to attack sooner than planned!" suggested Bhola Nath, urgently. "Else they'll get the better of us before we even strike." Shiv's ears pricked up. He didn't much care for this change of plans.

"I think you're right," the big man agreed. "They've already started swarming our tunnels. But how do we inform the rest about the change of plans? They will be waiting for another hour, and we need to act simultaneously for our plan to succeed."

"Where's your *puja* room, Indrajit?" asked Bhola Nath, face set in determination. A puzzled Indrajit guided them to an inside room. There, Bhola Nath picked up the conch shell found in every Bengali home, and ran up to the open terrace. And standing there gallantly, in full view of all, he blew on the conch shell with all his might and all his heart. The haunting sound of the conch shell filled the town air loud and clear, even going miles beyond.

Suddenly a shot rang out, and Bhola Nath crumpled to the ground, his limp hands still clutching the conch shell.

*"BHOLA NATH!!"* cried out Indrajit, as he rushed to his fallen leader. But the revolution was over for Bhola Nath as he lay lifeless.

Significantly, the call to freedom had been made. A minute later, hundred different conch shells, from hundred different parts of the town, answered the call. A few more gunshots were heard, and a few more cries of pain rang out. But the call of the conch shell increased in intensity and soon the entire town was totally covered by the inimitable sound.

The Great Revolution had truly begun.

*****

"As per our plans, we'll first take the arms depot," said Indrajit, the automatic new leader of the movement. Five of his lieutenants had gathered in one of the hundred tunnels, and were looking intently at him to give the orders. Along with his new authority, Indrajit's imposing personality placed him on a high pedestal amongst the men. Here was a man easy to respect and obey.

"The tunnel leading to the area just below the arms depot is ready," confirmed Chatterjee, the new second-in-command.

"Yes. So you first lead Group Five into the tunnel and blow up the depot. I'll be outside the depot with Groups One and Four, and take over whatever has not blown up. As we are attacking, Amit, with Groups Two and Three, will secure the perimeter of the depot and cover our backs. Remember, time is of essence here. Everyone should move at exactly the precise moment."

Shiv heard the plan as though in a dream. "Wh... what ab... about me?? Can I go now? Just an hour left for me to be in place?"

"No, it's too dangerous for you to be on your own," advised Indrajit. "You'd better stay close to me."

Shiv couldn't understand the logic. Here the big man was about to lead a revolution, and he thought it would be safer to stay near him? But he didn't have time to further worry about that. Chatterjee and his group had scurried away in another direction, through another tunnel.

"It'll take them ten minutes to reach the depot. Ten minutes for us to strike."

It gave Shiv ten minutes to reflect on the situation he was in. When the old man at Nizams had told him he could travel in time, he was overexcited at the prospect of seeing some of the most unimaginable things. He was confident that science and technology would be at a totally different level than the one in existence in the 21st century. He expected to see vehicles zooming at the speed of light... he expected the world to have colonised other planets... to have eradicated poverty and sickness from the face of this planet... he expected the common use of mysterious powers of levitation and even, invisibility... and total control over atoms, molecules and DNA.

He wanted to know what would happen in 2010 in 2020 and 2050. He wanted to read history books of these periods, and maybe even carry such books back home. He had hoped he could learn more about his own future. He wanted to know what mistakes he would make in his life and their consequences, so that when he returned home he could ensure he didn't make those mistakes. He wanted to know if he would ever befriend anybody, and not remain the loner he was. Oh, he wanted to know a hundred things, and more.

But here he was, in the middle of a revolution, and a million miles away from any answer.

"Okay, everyone ready?" Indrajit stood up, country-made guns in each hand. Country-made guns and common explosives, against the might of modern sophisticated weaponry! Shiv wondered what chance these brave people really had. He did not know that in a struggle such as this, faith in oneself and in one's ideology were the most powerful weapons.

Indrajit addressed the hundred people from Group One and Four that had gathered. "Remember, our duty is to make a charge right from here, and head towards the depot. We stop for no one! Even when the Chinese start shooting at us, we go on. Some of us will not reach our target, but hopefully, most will. Before we reach the depot, Chatterjee's group will have blown most of it up. We immediately take control of whatever is left. Once that is ours, we'll be able to fight back." He looked at his watch. "In another two minutes the depot should blow up. READY? *CHAAAARGE!!!*"

Before he knew it, Shiv was charging alongside Indrajit. They passed a few houses without the Chinese realising it. From another house, eighty-odd people from Groups Two and Three joined them. They remained a hundred metres behind the attack force.

Suddenly a Chinese patrol spotted them and immediately opened fire. It was not a Melter that they used, but another modern weapon. Out poured dozens of bombs from each barrel, each as small as a coin, but with the destructive power of a tank. Over a dozen of the first group were blown up in seconds. But the charge continued unabated.

And then they heard the blasts.

It stopped them in their tracks, despite their pledge to continue running. The depot must have been another half a kilometre away, but the heat from the blast scorched them all. It was an incredibly huge explosion, followed by a series of smaller blasts. They saw the smoke bellowing out as Indrajit raised his arm and cried out, *"Now my friends!! This is what you were waiting for! Let's finish this job. CHAAARGE!!"*

Indrajit urged his men to follow him as he ran at full pace. As they neared the burning depot they saw hundreds of Chinese running away from it.

"This is what we counted on," said Indrajit, looking pleased with himself. "There will be little resistance when we reach the depot. Hope Chatterjee and others have escaped unhurt."

"But won't the Chinese come back? They are much more heavily armed," said Shiv, running and looking around him in amazement. He wondered how his parents would react seeing him in this role... father would probably faint, and mother would surely suffer a heart attack.

They reached the burning depot and saw just a handful of Chinese trying to douse the fire. A short fight ensued, but the rebels quickly overpowered the Chinese.

"Spread out and quickly give me an account of what's gone up in flames, and what's left!" Indrajit ordered his two groups. "Groups Two and Three cordon off the area and hold your positions!"

The men moved as ordered and in minutes they had a report. "The central depot is totally destroyed. Two buildings on its left and another on its right are marginally destroyed. The arms and ammunitions in those buildings are intact."

"Good! Distribute those arms to Groups Two and Three, then collect whatever is left and stand alongside them."

"HURRY!!" called out the leader of Group Three. "The Chinese have regrouped and are about to counter-attack!"

The counter-attack did come, but it was a cautious one. The Chinese couldn't use the Melter, as they were scared of destroying the rest of their own depot. The revolutionaries suppressed the first attack, and by the time the second attack came they were rearmed with the sophisticated Chinese weapons. The Chinese were now at the receiving end.

The Revolution's first strike was a success.

*****

"Congratulations!" Shiv greeted Indrajit as they entered a room that was now their control room. "But what happens now? Surely the Chinese will call for reinforcements, and you all will get wiped out. It's just a matter of time."

"Maybe, but our message will have spread. The Chinese can be defeated. Our messengers have already gone to give the news to the neighbouring towns and villages. They have all been informed of what we are planning and what they could do. If this spark gets ignited amongst the people in these towns too and if they organise a counter-revolt now, then the Movement will be established. The Chinese will not find it easy to control its spread then."

"All that is great, but what about me?" wondered Shiv aloud. He checked his watch. "Only 30 minutes left! Can I please leave now??"

Suddenly Indrajit paled. "I forgot about that! But all the points must be guarded. You will not get ten feet from here before the Chinese get you."

A flustered Shiv started getting panicky. "But... but... my parents... they'll be petrified on finding me missing. And the next slot for returning may be centuries away."

"Let me think," said Indrajit, but instead started discussing battle plans with his lieutenants.

As the battle outside raged on, Shiv moved away from the control room and in a daze wandered about. He approached the area where the main depot had stood, minutes before. The building had totally been razed to the ground and fires were blazing at a number of sections. He suddenly roused himself. What was he doing just wandering about? He had to find a way to get out of here!

"The Elite Guard is here! And they are on their Fliers!" someone shouted from the front.

"WHAT? Already?" Indrajit rushed out of the conference. "That's not good. They are too well equipped and will get to us faster than expected."

Shiv looked up disbelievingly and saw 30 to 40 very smartly uniformed Chinese soldiers flying small vehicles. Controlling them like motorbikes, they zoomed down from above and attacked the rebels with small ray guns. In a few seconds, scores of rebels lay dead on the ground.

*"Take cover!!"* shouted Indrajit at the top of his voice. Most rebels ran for cover, which meant fewer people protecting the outer ring of the depot. The Chinese on the ground started breaking through the ring.

"I think we have lost," somebody said close by, It was Chatterjee.

*"Chatterjee!"* exclaimed Indrajit. "How did you manage to break away?"

"Through the same tunnel we used for blowing the depot. It's still hot and smoking, yet we managed to use it to give you a hand. But all for nothing, I see. We won't be able to hold this lot back."

And just as doom lay at their doorstep, someone once again shouted, *"It's the men from Bishnu Para!! And they are on the Chinese Fliers."*

The two teams of Fliers clashed in midair, even as the battle on the ground intensified. One of the Fliers from Bishnu Para landed in front of Indrajit.

*"Bapida!!"* cried Indrajit happily. "How did you manage to come so quickly?"

"We were totally prepared. The minute we heard your explosion we pounced on the squadron of Fliers in our town."

"Great! Now we are more evenly balanced... till at least their main reserves come."

"Maybe, but by then our brothers from other towns and villages will be here too."

Shiv was happy for the rebels but petrified about his own prospects. The Revolution was in full swing, diminishing his chances of returning by the minute. And now he had just 15 minutes. He saw more rebels emerging from the main building of the burning depot. "The rest of my team," explained Chatterjee, passing on to them sophisticated weapons they had recovered.

Suddenly an idea struck Shiv. He ran into the burning main building of the depot. If they can come out of the tunnel, he could go into the tunnel as well. Through the dense smoke he spotted the huge cavernous opening in the floor inside. Thick smoke was still bellowing out amidst sudden spurts of fire. Without another thought, he jumped into the hole. He silently prayed that he was not jumping from the frying pan into the fire.

*****

He landed on something hard and uneven and immediately stumbled over. The minute his hands and knees touched the ground he got burnt. Jumping up, he tried to run in a blind direction. And immediately banged into a hot wall, and burnt himself more. Tears streaming down his eyes because of the smoke, he felt the side of the hot wall in short gaps. He moved sideways, touching the wall and moving on, until he felt no wall. It must be the opening of the tunnel he was looking for. He entered it. Shortly the smoke thinned and he could see where he was. He was in a large tunnel, which branched out in many directions.

Praying to God and trusting his sense of direction, he selected one route and ran forward. Five minutes of a brisk run and he saw a short ladder. He went up it and opened a trap door just above it. It opened into a small house. A scared old woman, cringing behind a chair, started praying aloud as she saw him climb into the room. Not paying attention to her, Shiv went to a window and crouching low, peeped out.

He had bypassed the battle area by a good three hundred metres, and the roads here were deserted. He checked the time. Just seven minutes left for him to make it to the 'connector', the rusty cylinder that was his entry point here. Maybe, just maybe, he would make it.

He immediately stepped out and ran as fast as he could towards the direction he felt the connector was. He expected a shout and a shot from behind, but neither came. Everyone's attention was on the depot. He knew he still had to cover almost a kilometre, so he shifted gear to the maximum, and sprinted towards his goal as though the devil himself was on his tail. But being lame, he had his limitations. He had covered just half the distance when he noticed that just two minutes were left. He could now see the rusted metal enclosure that was his gateway to returning home, but with a sickening feeling he knew he could never reach it in two minutes.

He was panting for breath but kept running, hoping against hope that his 'window' would remain open till he reached it.

Far away behind him, he heard a cry, "Someone's running away!"

The alarm had been sounded and five seconds later a Flier was hovering above his head, and an Elite Guard pointing a strange looking gun at him.

"That's it!" said Shiv to himself, stopping in mid-stride, mentally and physically defeated.

But even as he was about to give himself up, an idea struck him. He raised his arms in a show of surrender. The Chinese zoomed down and checked him for hidden arms. He was dressed in a parade suit, all with polished shoes and buckle and white arm-length gloves. He quickly handcuffed Shiv.

"Get on behind me," he commanded confidently, as he climbed onto his Flier and started the engine. Shiv climbed behind him and checked his watch for the umpteenth time.

Just one minute left! Time for action!

Just as the Elite Guard was revving the engine and turning his vehicle to return to the town, Shiv leaned forward and locked his handcuffed hands on the handle. It was pointing straight towards the connector. Taken totally by surprise, it took the Chinese a good five seconds to react. But that was enough for the super-fast vehicle to cover almost half the required distance to the connector. In one swift movement the Chinese broke Shiv's hold, and turned around to tackle him. He jerked his elbow back and hit Shiv squarely on his face. But, sitting behind, Shiv had a distinct advantage. A few seconds of struggle, and the vehicle was above the connector, and a surprised Slim Chang.

Shiv immediately broke off. Again the Elite guard was caught off-guard. He instantly stalled the engine and hovering at a height of about 20 feet, he turned around and caught Shiv by the shirt collar.

Fifteen seconds left! No time for a fight!

Shiv twisted away from the Chinese's hold and jumped. His hands cuffed, he landed awkwardly. A shooting pain ran up his right leg, his longer leg, as he realised he had twisted his ankle. But he was just ten feet from his goal. Standing between him and that goal was Slim Chang.

*"Stop him!!"* cried the Elite Guard, himself screeching his Flier to the ground and dismounting, all in one motion.

Tall Slim spread his arms and legs instantly. Behind Shiv the charging Elite Guard was just an arms length away. Less than five seconds left. So near, yet so far.

Just one last chance left.

Shiv dived between Slim's long legs. Slim grabbed at him and managed to hold him by the foot. Shiv squirmed and got through free. In a flash he half stood up behind Slim, who was left holding a shoe. Shiv saw the two Chinese charging at him, and made the final leap, head first, into the rusted metal connector. Just as his body entered the enclosure, and he was still in mid-air, he felt the Elite Guard's hand tightly grasp him by the foot.

The next instant, there was a loud explosion, followed by a blinding light and in its midst, he completed his dive.

*****

When he opened his eyes again, he was in the cabin at Nizams. When Shiv tried getting up, he cringed with pain. The swing doors of the cabin flung open and the old man looked in.

"Whew!! Looks like you are returning from hell."

"Worse. Much worse," answered Shiv, limping heavily he reached for the nearest chair in the main hall of the restaurant, and sat down.

"What's that?" asked the old man pointing to his foot.

Shiv looked down and was surprised to see a white glove around his ankle. It must be the Elite Guard's, he surmised. After grabbing Shiv by the foot, it must have been wrenched out of his hands as Shiv himself was hurtled through the time zone. He picked it up with both his hands. Another souvenir.

"Why are you handcuffed? And what happened to your shoe? And, more important, what happened to your face?" asked the old man with a mischievous smile.

"It's a long story *Chacha,* a very long story. But how do I get these handcuffs off?"

"A regular handcuff could have been cut open by the local blacksmith. But I can see this is no ordinary metal. It will not be easy getting out of it."

"But... but... how will I explain it to my family?" asked Shiv frantically, trying hard to pull his burnt hand out of this physical bondage.

"I never said these trips were easy," said the old man, still smiling.

"I must be leaving now," said Shiv, getting up. Gingerly he put his right leg on the ground and limped his way out of the restaurant.

"Come again," he heard the old man say.

Still panting from his recent run with a sprained ankle, bruised and battered on the face, his hands singed and cuffed to an unbreakable shackle, a broken Shiv stepped out of the restaurant with only one shoe, and headed homewards. Such a long, long trip he had made, and gained nothing from it. He didn't see the progress in science and technology that he hoped to see, and he didn't learn anything about the immediate future he and his world were to face.

It was already dark and he had a long way to go home. Good, he consoled himself. That would give him the time to think of an excuse for his parents about his sorry condition.

As he limped, Shiv promised himself, "It will be some time before I'll be hungry for *kathi rolls* again."

❑❑❑

# Children Story Books

Tales of
Gopal the Jester

More Tales of
Gopal the Jester

Big size, PP: 56 (In 4 colour), both the books also available in Hindi.

## Animal Folk Tales from Around the World (in 3 volumes)

Animal Folk Tales from Around the World Vol. 2 — 36/-

Big size Pages: 24 each (In 4 colour), Also available in Hindi

Witty Tales of
Tenali Rama
PP: 56 (In 2 colour)

Tales of
Tenali Rama
PP: 60 (In 2 colour)

Demy size
Pages: 104

Big size both the books also available in Hindi.

***Postage: Rs. 10/- each book. Every subsequent book: Rs. 5/- extra***